Theodore Thornton Munger

On the Threshold

Sixteenth Edition

Theodore Thornton Munger

On the Threshold
Sixteenth Edition

ISBN/EAN: 9783337397906

Printed in Europe, USA, Canada, Australia, Japan

Cover: Foto ©Andreas Hilbeck / pixelio.de

More available books at **www.hansebooks.com**

ON THE THRESHOLD.

BY

THEODORE T. MUNGER.

"Many men that stumble at the threshold."

SIXTEENTH EDITION.

BOSTON:
HOUGHTON, MIFFLIN AND COMPANY.
New York: 11 East Seventeenth Street.
The Riverside Press, Cambridge.
1885.

PREFACE.

THE object of this little book is to put into clear form some of the main principles that enter into life as it is now opening before young men in this country. Its suggestions are more specific and direct than if they had been addressed to older persons; still, I have aimed to support every point by sound reasons, and to join the authority and inspiration of the greater minds with my own views. I think I may assure my readers that they will not encounter a simple mass of advice, nor the generalities of an essay, but rather a series of hints suitable to the times, and pointing out paths that are just now somewhat obscured. If they find some pages that are strenuous in their suggestions, they will find none that are keyed to impossible standards of conduct, or filled with moralizings that are remote from the every-day business of life.

It is not pleasant to play the *rôle* of Polonius, and I undertake it only because Laertes seems to be quite as much in need of advice as ever. I have not, however, written out of a critical mood, so much as from a desire to bring young men face to face with the inspiring influences that, in a peculiar degree, surround them. The country was never so prosperous, the future never so full of happy assurance as it is to-day. To point out the way of reaping the double harvest of this prosperity and a noble manhood, is the motive that underlies these pages.

CONTENTS.

———◆———

I.

PURPOSE

I.

PURPOSE.

In entering upon this series of essays, or talks with young men, I wish to have it understood at the outset that I do not undertake to cover or even touch the whole truth of the subject in hand. The philosophical basis and the religious application will not be much regarded; hence, to some they may seem to lack profound thought, and to others moral earnestness; but I shall not mind if I can lead my readers to think seriously of what I do say. If I speak the truth, it will have enough philosophy in it; if it is carefully heeded, it will of itself grow into the moral and religious.

I begin with *Purpose*, because it naturally underlies the themes that are to follow, and also because it is a matter of special importance. I say *special* because I think that just now many young men are entering life without any very definite purpose; as some one has put it, "the world is full of purposeless people." It is due in part to nearly ten years of hard times, when occupations have been closed up, and multitudes of young men could find little to do. Business men have struggled along as best they could, capitalists have been idle, and young men have been shut up to the few chance openings, without much choice based on fitness or desire. It is also due to the fact that, during the previous years, large and sudden accumulations of property were made by people not accustomed to its use. The consciousness of wealth is always dangerous. When a young man comes to feel that because his father has wealth he has no need of personal exertion, he is doomed. Only the rarest natural gifts and the most exceptional training can save the sons of the rich from failure of the true ends of life. They may escape vice and attain to respectability, but for the most part they are hurt in some degree or respect. The consciousness of wealth in the latter part of life, after one has earned or become prepared for it, may be not only not injurious, but healthful, though one ought to be able to live a high and happy life without it. But anything that lessens in a young man the feeling that he is to make his own way in the world is hurtful to the last degree.

As the result of these two causes, — with others, doubtless, — young men of the present years, as a class, are not facing life with that resolute and definite purpose that is essential both to manhood and to external success. There is far less of this early measurement and laying hold of life with some definite intent than there was a generation ago. It is to be feared that we could not again fight the war for the Union to the same issue. Young men do not so much go to college as they are sent. They do not push their way into callings, but suffer themselves to be led into them. Indeed, the sacred word *calling* seems to have lost its meaning ; they hear no voice summoning them to the appointed field, but drift into this or that, as happens. They appear to be waiting, — to be floating with the current instead of rowing up the stream towards the hills where lie the treasures of life. I mean, of course, that this seems to be the drift, — not that it is a deliberate purpose.

My object is to interrupt this tendency, — to induce you to aim at a far end rather than a near one; to live under a purpose rather than under impulse; to set aside the thought of enjoyment, and get to thinking of attainment; to conceive of life as a race instead of a drift.

Men may be divided in many ways, but there is no clearer cut division than between those who have a purpose and those who are without one. It is the character of the purpose that determines the character of the man, — for a purpose may be good or bad, high or low. It is the strength and definiteness of the purpose that determine the measure of success.

It is one of the gracious features of our nature that we are capable of forming high and noble purposes. The mind overleaps its ignorance, and fixes upon what is wisest and best. A child is always planning noble things before its "life fades into the light of the common day." There may not always be congruity in these early ambitions, but they are nearly always noble. A friend of mine set out in life with the complex purpose of becoming " a great man, a good man, and a stage-driver." He has not yet achieved greatness, and I doubt if he has ever held a four-in-hand or knows

what *tandem* means, except in its Latin
sense; but he has not failed in the other
part, being the worthy pastor of a church,
over which he presides with a dignity and
wisdom that are the proper outcome of his
early conceptions. The weaker element
naturally passed away, and the nobler ones
took up his expanding powers.

Nor does this distinction divide men according to good and bad; for, while an
aimless man cannot be said to be good, he
may cherish a very definite aim without
ranking amongst the virtuous. Few men
ever held to a purpose more steadily than
Warren Hastings, having for the dream
and sole motive of his youth and manhood
to regain the lost estates and social position
of his family; but he can hardly be classed
amongst good men. He is a fine example,
however, of how a clearly conceived purpose strengthens and inspires a man. The
career of Beaconsfield — the most brilliant
figure amongst modern English statesmen
— is another illustration of how a definite
purpose carries a man on to its fulfillment.
When the young Jew was laughed and
jeered into silence in his first attempt to
address the House of Commons, he re-

marked, " The time will come when you will hear me ; " speaking not out of any pettishness of the moment, but from a settled purpose to lead his compeers. The rebuff but whetted the edge of his grand ambition.

I do not mean to say that a purpose, if cherished with sufficient energy, will always carry a man to its goal, — for every man has his limitations, — but rather that it is sure to carry him on towards some kind of success; often it proves greater than that aimed at. Shakespeare went down to London to retrieve his fortune, — a very laudable purpose ; but the ardor with which he sought it unwittingly ended in the greatest achievements of the human intellect. Saul determined to crush out Christianity ; but the energy of his purpose was diverted to the opposite and immeasurably nobler end. It would be absurd for me to assure you that if you aim and strive with sufficient energy to become great statesmen, or the heads of corporations, or famous poets or artists, or for any other specific high end, you will certainly reach it. For though there are certain great prizes that any man may win who will pay the

price, there are others that are reserved
for the few who are peculiarly fortunate,
or have peculiar claims. The Providence
that, blindly to us, endows and strangely
leads, apportions the great honors of existence; but Providence has nothing good or
high in store for one who does not resolutely aim at something high and good.
A purpose is the eternal condition of success. Nothing will take its place. Talent
will not; nothing is more common than
unsuccessful men of talent. Genius will
not; unrewarded genius is a proverb; the
" mute, inglorious Milton " is not a poetic
creation. The chance of events, the push
of circumstances, will not. The natural unfolding of faculties will not. Education
will not; the country is full of unsuccessful
educated men; indeed, it is a problem of
society what to do with the young men it
is turning out of its colleges and professional schools. There is no road to success
but through a clear, strong purpose. A
purpose underlies character, culture, position, attainment of whatever sort. Shakespeare says: " Some achieve greatness, and
some have greatness thrust upon them;'
but the latter is external, and not to be ac-
counted as success.

It is worth while to look into the reasons of the matter a little.

(1.) A purpose, steadily held, trains the faculties into strength and aptness.

The first main thing a man has to do in this world is to turn his possibilities into powers, or to get the *use* of himself. Here we are packed full of faculties, — physical, mental, moral, social, — with almost no instincts, and therefore no natural use of them ; a veritable box of tools, ready for use. Think what a capability is lodged in the hand of the pianist or of the physician, — fairly seeing with his fingers. Or take the mechanical eye, instantly seizing proportions ; or the ear of the musician ; or the mind bending itself to mathematical problems, or grouping wide arrays of facts for induction, — the every-day work of the professional man, the merchant, and the manufacturer. How to use these tools — how to get the faculties at work — is the main question. The answer is, *steady use under a main purpose.*

The call to-day is not only for educated, but for trained men. The next mightiest event that daily happens in this world of ours, after the sunrise, — that " daily miracle," as Edwin Arnold calls it, — is the publication of such a newspaper as the " New York Herald " or " London Times." If it were possible to send to Mars or Jupiter a single illustration of our highest achievements, it should be a copy of a great Daily. I think nothing finer could be brought back. But what produces this superb and gigantic achievement three hundred and more times a year ? Not learning, talent, energy, nor money, but training. From the editor-in-chief, with his frequent leaders, — broad, compact, trenchant, — and the manager, bringing together the various departments in just proportion and harmony, so that the paper goes from the press almost like the solar system in its adjusted balance, down to the folding and distributing departments, the work throughout is done by men trained to their specific tasks by steady and sympathetic habit.

Every man's work should be both an inspiration and a trade ; that is, he should love it, and he should have that facility in it that comes from use. It is said that Napoleon could go through the manual of the common soldier better than any man in his armies. He would not have been the greatest general had he not been the best soldier, his genius would have been weak without the support of the drill and the practical knowledge of all the details of the military. So of railroading, now one of the great callings; it has become a nearly universal custom that every higher position shall be filled from below by promotion, according to excellence, and this excellence turns upon two points: an intelligent and sympathetic interest in the work, and consequent handiness in it. One cannot look over a company of railroad men without perceiving that those highest up have the most *head* for the entire business. I have noticed, in looking at machinery, that the proprietor can explain it better than the workman who operates it.

All lines of business are conducted more and more upon the principle of promotion. Less and less do men step from one occupation to another. The demand is for *trained* men. But life is too short and the standards are too severe for various trainings. It is seldom one is found who has thoroughly fitted himself for diverse pursuits. Our aptitudes are not many. Pick out the successful man in almost any occupation, and nearly without exception it will be found he has been trained to it.

(2.) Life is cumulative in all ways. A steady purpose is like a river, that gathers volume and momentum by flowing on. The successful man is not one who can do many things indifferently, but one thing in a superior manner. Versatility is overpraised. There is a certain value in having many strings to one's bow, but there is more value in having a bow and a string, a hand and an eye, that will every time send the arrow into the bull's-eye of the target. The world is full of vagabonds who can turn their hands to anything. The man who does odd jobs is not the one who gets very far up in any job. The *factotum* is a convenience, but he is seldom a success. The machinist who works in anywhere is not the one who is put to the nicest work. A certain concentration is essential to excellence, except in rare cases like Leonardo da Vinci, and Pascal, and Aristotle, and Franklin, whose natures were so broad as to cover all studies and pursuits. One of the most extensive wool-buyers in the world says that his success is due to the fact that his father and grandfather handled wool, that his own earliest recollections were of handling wool, and that he had kept on handling it. The largest manufacturer of paper in the country is the son of a paper-maker, born and bred to all the details of the business. There are, indeed, many cases of large success where men have passed from one pursuit to another, but in most you will find a certain unity running through their various occupations. One may begin a stone-cutter and end as a geologist, like Hugh Miller, or a sculptor, like Powers; or as a machinist, and turn out an inventor; or as a printer, and become a publisher. A strong definite purpose is many-handed, and lays hold of whatever is near that can serve it; it has a magnetic power that draws to itself whatever is kindred.

(3.) A purpose, by holding one down to some steady pursuit and legitimate occupation, wars against the tendency to engage in ventures and speculations. The devil of the business world is *chance*. Chance is chaotic; it belongs to the period

> " When eldest Night
> And Chaos, ancestors of Nature, held
> Eternal anarchy amidst the noise
> Of endless wars, and by confusion stood."

It is opposed in nature to order and law; it is the abdication of reason, the enthronement of guess. The chance element in business is not only demoralizing to the man, but in the long run it is disastrous to his fortunes. And if it yields a temporary success it is a success unearned, and therefore unappreciated; for we must put something of thought and genuine effort into an enterprise before we can get any substantial good out of it. The defalcations, the shoddy of society, the diamonds gleaming on unwashed hands, the ignorance that looks through plate-glass, and no small part of the crime that looks through iron bars, are the creations of the chance or speculative element in business. No good ever comes from it. If it lifts a man up, it is only to dash him to the earth. In California they aptly call it "playing with the tiger," and the game always ends by the tiger eating the man. The chances in the stock market of San Francisco are less than in Chinese gambling, at which the Caucasian affects to laugh; but the Mongolian plays to better purpose with his one chance in ten than does the other in the ever-recurring bonanza. The Californians are not yet a rich people; but almost every old resident has at some time held a fortune in his hands. Their speculations are very like their smelting of quicksilver, — going up an expansive vapor, but trickling back solid into a single reservoir. If there is one purpose a young man needs to hold to rigidly and without exception, it is to keep to legitimate modes of business. Don't abjure your reason by appealing to chance, nor insult order by taking up that which, as Milton says, " by confusion stands." Don't of deliberate purpose make a figure of yourself for " the spirits of the wise sitting in the clouds to laugh at." A steady purpose embodied in a substantial pursuit shuts out these chance forms of business. Question the men of substantial character and fortune, and you will find that they have avoided the illegitimate in business, and have held fast to some steady line of pursuit, — busy in prosperous times and patiently waiting in hard times. The last ten years have witnessed a bravery and sagacity worthy of highest admiration, — men conducting business year after year without profit or at a loss, keeping up their relations with the business world, carrying along their employees, exercising forbearance with less fortunate creditors, nursing the dull embers of their unremunerative business instead of petulantly suffering them to go out. The previous ten years showed us the heroism of war; but these ten years of stagnation have revealed the heroism of peace, and these brave, patient waiters upon fortune are now reaping their reward, while those who gave up and turned to this and that are out of the ranks of our great army of prosperity.

It may seem from what I have said that I would advise young men to concentrate their entire energies upon a pursuit, and forget all else. But I am very far from doing that.

The most fundamental mistake men make is in not recognizing the breadth of their nature, and a consequent working of some single part of it. One must give play to his whole nature and fill out all his relations, or he will have a poor ending. He must heed the social, domestic, and religious elements of his being, as well as the single one that yields him a fortune. These should be embraced under a *purpose* as clear and strong as that which leads to wealth, and be cherished, not out of a bare sense of duty, but for manly completeness. The most pitiable sight one ever sees is a young man doing nothing; the furies early drag him to his doom. Hardly less pitiable is a young man doing but one thing,— his whole being centred on money or fame —forgetful of the broad world of intellectual capacity within him, of the broader and sweeter world of social and domestic life, and of the infinite world of the spirit that inspires him on every side, and holds his destinies, whether he knows it or not. It is not only quite possible, but an easy and natural thing, for a young man fronting life to say, I will make the most of myself; I will recognize my whole nature; I will neglect no duty that belongs to all men; I will carry along with an even and just hand those relations that make up a full manhood.

I find four general purposes that should enter into the plan of every man's life as essential to its completeness. Hereafter I shall speak more definitely; now only of fundamental or leading purposes.

(1.) A young man should have an employment congenial, if possible, and as near as may be to the line of pursuit he intends to follow. I have anticipated much that might be said here. The choice of a profession or occupation is a hard one to handle practically or speculatively. So many are forced into work, and take that nearest at hand, so many drift into an occupation because the time has come; so many are set to work too early for choice, that few seem left who can make a careful selection. It is a sad thing that any should be defrauded of this natural prerogative. It may be quite right to train a boy to a calling, but never to the exclusion of his personal choice; if for the ministry, and he deliberately prefers to become a machinist, or a farmer, or an editor, it must be suffered. A call, or calling, is a divine thing, and must be obeyed. Pitt was trained from his earliest years for the great place he filled, but for the most part great men have chosen for themselves. But one should settle the matter only after very thorough consideration. Dr. Bushnell once said to a young man who was consulting him on this point, "Grasp the handle of your being," — a most significant and profound piece of advice. There is in every one a taste or fitness that is as a handle to the faculties; if one gets hold of it, he can work the entire machinery of his being to the best advantage. Before committing one's self to a pursuit, one should make a very thorough exploration of himself, and get down to the core of his being. The fabric of one's life should rest upon the central and abiding qualities of one's nature, —else it will not stand. Hence a choice should be based on what is within rather than be drawn from without. Choose your employment because you like it, and not because it has some external promise. The "good opening" is in the man, —not in circumstances. An ill-adaptation will nullify any good promise, while aptitude creates success. All true life and success are from within. God so made the world and all things in it, —"seed within itself" is the eternal law. I do not mean that every boy has an inborn taste for some specific work, —type-setting, or blacksmithing, or editing. Aptitudes are generic; if one follows his general taste he will probably succeed in several kindred pursuits. While we cannot well go contrary to nature, there is a certain play and oscillation of our faculties, — as of the planets that yet keep to the appointed journey. The mechanical eye covers a large variety of employments. A spirit of ministration is fundamental to at least two of the great professions. One of an intensely reflective disposition should not make existence a long battle by binding himself to a life of external activity; and many a man pines and shrivels in the study who would exult in a life upon the soil. But having got into some occupation or line of pursuit that is fairly congenial, running in the direction of your inmost taste and aptitude, hold fast to it. If it is altogether distasteful after fair trial, throw it aside, and start again. No one can row against the stream all his life and make a success of it. It is fundamental that there should be in the main accord between the man and his work. I do not mean that one is absolutely to do the same thing — shove the plane, beat the anvil, tend the loom, measure land, sell goods — to the end, but that he should continue in the same general department, — thus utilizing previous aptness and experience. The work first undertaken may be too restricting ; one should be always looking for its higher forms. One may climb by a steady purpose as well

as by a persistent iteration of the same
thing, but it must be in a related field of
effort. Successful life is commonly of one
piece; and it comes of intelligent purpose,
— never by chance.

(2.) Having thus settled into some fair
line of pursuit, the next main purpose
should be to get a home of one's own.
Every young man expects to marry, and
this expectation ought to carry with it the
definite thought of a home, — a thing not
realized under any boarding or renting system.

I put this among the fundamental purposes simply because it is such. Character,
happiness, destiny, turn on its realization.
It is the main safeguard against immorality. It is essential to a development of,
the whole nature. It is the chief source of
sound and abiding happiness. It is the surest defense against evil fortune. When
once a home has been secured, abject poverty almost never follows. Man is like the
animals in that his first need is a place in
which to hide his head. Indeed, a home
sums up life; outside of it, it is meagre and
partial. In the home every worthy purpose
finds realization. It is the objective point

in existence, — a home beyond and a home here. Hence it should not only mingle in one's dreams as among the probabilities, but should enter in amongst the distinct purposes. " A home of my own," — no phrase of English words is so sweet as that. A bit of ground where you can plant a rose and hope to pluck its blossoms as the summers come and go; a roof that shall be your shelter for tender dependents; a spot of earth and a house owned, and so ministering to that deep call for a resting place natural to us all; a home to hold loved ones while they live, and to enshrine their memory when they are gone; the goal of labors, the sanctuary of the affections, the gateway into and out of the world, — a thing so central and large as this should enter into one's plans with sharp and strong purpose.

(3.) Another central purpose should be to become a good citizen. This is not so trite a point as it seems. The moralizing on our relation to government that abounds in literature and common speech chiefly refers to subjects rather than to citizens. Obedience and loyalty are old virtues; citizenship is comparatively a new thing, of which we have yet hardly a full conception.

To obey as subjects is a duty very well understood; to govern as citizens is a complex
act, involving the two duties of obedience
and ruling.   The Sovereign People is a vast
and significant phrase.   If we were to speculate upon it, we should find that it involves the highest function of man; for man
reaches the perfection of his nature when
obedience and sway are perfectly coördinated, — that is, when he has learned to
obey and to rule, doing each perfectly.   To
overcome and sit in an eternal throne is the
highest glimpse of revealed destiny.   It is
something very grand and inspiring — if we
will think of it — that our country puts
upon us as citizens this sum and end of all
duties; that citizenship is in the direct
line of eternal destiny.   It is an adjustment
of the political and the spiritual that marks
the coming of the kingdom of heaven.   One
of the thoughts to which a young man
should school himself is that he is an actual
part of the government.   Good citizenship
thus becomes an inalienable duty, an obli-
gation springing from the nature of things.
When one is so related to the state he cannot see a law broken, or a public trust
abused, or an office perverted, without a

sense of personal wrong. The great Louis said, " I am France," but every American citizen can say, " I am the state." By good citizenship I do not mean necessarily a mingling in what is technically named politics, though one must not hold one's self aloof from the details of citizenship, but rather that the public welfare should weigh steadily on every man's heart and conscience ; as it was the duty of every Roman to " see to it that no harm came to the republic."

I place good citizenship amongst the fundamental aims, because it represents a feeling that is central to character. One cannot avoid it without self-injury. It leaves a man exposed to the absorption of his private business, and so to that selfishness and narrowness that comes from a limited range of interests. Exclusive devotion to the home makes one weak ; to business, selfish. A hearty and practical interest in the state alone can make one strong and large.

(4.) After one has well settled himself in these three main relations, — employment, home, country, — all other general purposes may be summed up in the one word *culture ;* or, as this is a somewhat derided and over-

used word at present, I will put it otherwise
— resolve to make the most of yourself.
Still that word *culture* is the best. *Cultivate* yourself; I do not mean in the sense of
putting on a finish, but of feeding the roots
of your being, strengthening your capacities, nourishing whatever is good, repress-
ing whatever is bad. Determine that not a
power shall go to waste; that every faculty
shall do its utmost and reach its highest.
I say to you with all carefulness, the noblest sight this world offers is a young man
bent upon making the most of himself.
Alas that so many seem not to care what
they become; men in stature, but not yet
born into a world of purpose and attainment,
— babes in their comprehension of life! A
cigar, a horse, a flirtation, a suit of clothes, a
night of drinking, a low theatrical or dance,
and just enough work to attain such things,
or got without work, — how the spirits of
the wise, sitting in the clouds, laugh at
them! What an introduction to manhood
and manly duties! One cannot start thus
in life, and make himself master of it, or get
any real good out of it. A part of his folly
may ooze out as the burdens of life press on
him, and necessity may drive him to sober

labor, but he will halt and stumble to the end. It is a sad thing to begin life with low conceptions of it. There is no misfortune comparable to a youth without a sense of nobility. Better be born blind than not see the glory of life. It is not, indeed, possible for a young man to measure life, but it is possible to cherish that lofty and sacred enthusiasm which the dawn of life awakens. It is possible to say, — I am resolved to put life to its noblest and best use.

If I could get the ear of every young man for but one word, it would be this: *Make the most and the best of yourself.* There is no tragedy like wasted life, — life failing of its end, — life turned to a false end.

The true way to begin life is not to look off upon it to see what it offers, but to take a good look at self. Find out what you are, how you are made up, your capacities and lacks, and then determine to get the most out of yourself possible. Your faculties are avenues between the good of the world and yourself; the larger and more open they are, the more of it you will get. Your object should be to get all the riches and sweetness of life into yourself; the method is through trained faculties. You find your self a mind: teach it to think, to work broadly and steadily, to serve your needs pliantly and faithfully. You find in yourself social capacities: make yourself the best citizen, the best friend and neighbor, the kindest son and brother, the truest husband and father. Whatever you are capable of in these directions, that be and do. Let nothing within you go to waste. You also find in yourself moral and religious faculties. Beware lest you suffer them to lie dormant, or but summon them to brief periodic activity. No man can make the most of himself who fails to train this side of his nature. Deepen and clarify your sense of God. Gratify by perpetual use the inborn desire for communion with Him. Listen evermore to conscience. Keep the heart soft and responsive to all sorrow. Love with all love's divine capacity and quality. And above all let your nature stretch itself towards that sense of infinity that comes with the thought of God. There is nothing that so deepens and amplifies the nature as the use of it in moral and spiritual ways. One cannot make the most of one's self who leaves it out.

If these general purposes are resolutely

followed, they are sure to yield as much of success as is possible in each given case.

A pursuit followed in its main drift; a home to contain the life; good citizenship as the sum of public duties; culture, or making the most of one's self, as the sum of personal and religious duties, — these are the four winds of inspiration that should blow through the heart of a young man; these are the foundations of that city of character and destiny which, when built, lies four-square, — Work, Home, Humanity, and Self, as made in the image of God and for God.

II.

FRIENDS AND COMPANIONS.

'God divided man into men that they might help each other."— SENECA.

"A man that hath friends must show himself friendly."— SOLOMON.

" A talent is perfected in solitude ; a character in the stream of the world." — GOETHE.

"Live with wolves, and you will learn to howl." — SPANISH PROVERB.

" Although unconscious of the pleasing charm,
The mind still bends where friendship points the way ;
    Let virtue then thy partner's bosom warm,
Lest vice should lead thy softened soul astray."
                    THEOGNIS, *from Xenophon.*

II.

FRIENDS AND COMPANIONS.

WITHOUT doubt, home and companions are the chief external influences that determine character. One is nearly always good, because it is charged with divine instincts; the other is uncertain in its character, because it springs out of the chances of the world. The main feature of the home is love which "works no ill;" hence its natural influence is favorable to good character. Parents for the most part inculcate truth, purity, honesty, and kindness. With abundant allowance for mistake and neglect, the influence of parents and brother and sister is good, but outside of the home there is no such certainty.

When John bids father and mother good by amongst the Berkshire hills, and goes to Boston or New York to make his way in the world, his future depends with almost mathematical certainty upon the character of his

3

associates. He may have good principles and high purposes; tender words of advice are in his ears; his Bible lies next his heart, and love follows him with unceasing prayers; but John will do well or ill as he falls amongst good or bad companions. Education, ingrafted principles and tastes, remembered love, ambition, conscience, — all these will do much for him, but they will not avail against this later influence.

There are many turning-points when the question of success or failure is decided again and again. Life is a campaign, in which a series of fortresses are to be taken; all previous victories and advances may be thrown away by failure in the next. Nearly the last of these is companionship; if one wins the victory here, the reward of a prosperous manhood is within his reach.

At the risk of logically inverting my subject, I will speak first of friendship; and I must beg your patience while I put a foundation under my suggestions.

If there were but one general truth that I could lodge in the mind of any one or all men, it would be this: that *true life consists in the fulfillment of relations.* We are born into relations; we never get out of them all duty consists in meeting them. The family, the church, the state, the humanity at large, — these are the sources of our primary and abiding duties, as well as of our happiness, — the sum-total of ethics and religion.

The relation of friends, though not so sharply defined as that of the family or the state, is as real and as essential to a full life. Emerson says : " Maugre all the selfishness that chills like east winds the world, the whole human family is bathed with an element of love like a fine ether." To get this ensphering love into form and expression is the office of friendship. Bacon goes so far as to say that " a principal fruit of friendship is the ease and discharge of the fullness of the heart." He goes on in his noble and wise way to name its other points, and nothing on the subject is better than his threefold statement of its uses : " Peace in the affections, support of the judgment, and bearing a part in all actions and occasions."

It is not enough to love only our own family. Love is a great and wide passion, demanding various food and broad fields to range in. When one is only " a family man " he may have a sound nature, but it will not be a large or generous one ; and he will shrink rather than expand with years, and sink into the inevitable sadness that attends old age.

Nor is Bacon's second point of less importance, — to aid one's judgment. Advice can hardly come from any other than a friend when the question involves grave issues. A stranger is not sufficiently interested, a relative is blinded by excess of love, but a friend's advice is tempered by affection, while it is not overruled by the imperativeness of natural instinct. There is much wisdom in the every-day words, " As a friend I advise you," for no other can advise so well.

Bacon's third point — friends as helpers on all occasions — does not have its full weight until we learn that late lesson that man is not equal to life. There is more to do than one can do alone, and an unfriended life will be poor and meagre. It is an old saying that " a friend is another himself." If, as a mere matter of strength and resource, I were to face life with the choice of either a fortune or friends, I would be wiser to choose the latter as more helpful

Of course I regard friendship as a real and abiding thing, and not as that other thing that comes and goes with fortune. I have no faith in the miserable notions that the poor are friendless because they are poor, and that friends desert on the approach of poverty. Poverty may winnow the false from the true, but it does not destroy the wheat. The poor may be friendless, and even poor because they are friendless, never having won friends. This fine relation does not turn upon poverty, but upon disposition, or temper, or the chances of life. Happy is he who wins friends in early life by true affinities! He multiplies himself; he has more hands and feet than his own, and other fortresses to flee into when his own are dismantled by evil fortune, and other hearts to throb with his joy.

Friendship is of such a nature that it is difficult to name rules for it; it is its own law and method. So ethereal a thing cannot be brought under choice or rule. It is rather a matter of destiny. If one is born to have friends he will have them. Emerson says that one need not seek for friends; they come of themselves. But Solomon goes deeper in his proverb: " A man that hath friends must show himself friendly." Let one offer to the world a large, generous, true, sympathetic nature, and, rich or poor, he will have friends, and he will never be friendless whatever catastrophes befall him.

Not as giving rules, but rather touching the matter in the way of suggestion, I will name a few points that it is well to think of : —

(1.) Cultivate the friendly spirit. If one would have friends he must be worthy of them. The bright plumage and the songs of birds are designed to win their mates. It is in vain for one to say, I want friends ; I will go seek them. Go within rather, and establish yourself in friendly sympathy with your fellow-men ; learn to love ; get the helpful spirit, and above all the responsive temper, and friends will come to you as birds fly to their beautiful singing mates.

(2.) Make friends early in life, else you will never have them. Youth is often moody, and keeps by itself. The very intensity with which it wakes up to individuality drives it into solitariness, where it morbidly feasts on the wonderful fact of selfhood. There is danger also lest we be caught by entertaining companions instead of winning congenial friends, and so start in life with a set of mere associates. It is only in the first third of our three-score and ten that life-long friends are made. Agreeable associations may be formed later, and now and then a friendship when there is great congeniality and freshness of spirit; but friendship is a union and mingling, a shaping of plastic substances to each other that cannot be effected after the mould of life has hardened. We may touch hereafter, but not mingle.

(3.) Hold fast to your friends. It is one of the commonest regrets in after-life that early friendships were not kept up. Change of residence, neglect of correspondence or of holiday courtesies, some divergence of taste or belief or outward condition, — for some such cause a true friendship is often suffered to languish and die out. Shakespeare well says : —

> " I count myself in nothing else so happy
> As in a soul rememb'ring my good friends."

And again in Hamlet : —

> "The friends thou hast, and their adoption tried,
> Grapple them to thy soul! with hoops of steel."

(4.) Make a point of having friends

amongst your elders. Friendship between those of the same age is sweeter, but friendship with elders is more useful, or, rather, they supplement each other. One is the wine of life; the other is its food. The latter balances life, and brings the good of all periods down into one. It is one of the divinest features of human life that in this way there is no such thing as solitary youth or solitary age. Youth may get the value, if not the reality, of the wisdom of age, and age keep forever young. Theology and poetry assert eternal youth; it is neither a dogma of one nor a dream of the other, but a logical realization of human sympathy and love. There is nothing more detestable in American society than the drawing off of young people into a society of their own, — young people's parties and children's parties! There is not only a strong flavor of vulgarity in it, but positive loss on both sides.

(5.) Avoid having many confidants. It is weak; it breeds trouble. Secrets are not in themselves good things, but when of necessity they exist their nature should be respected. Having them, it is well to keep them. Avoid also the effusive habit. It is

pitiable to see a man pouring himself out
into every listening ear, — mind and heart
and body inverted, the girdle of selfhood
thrown aside, and all the secret ways of the
being laid open for the common foot. It
is a violation of identity, a squandering of
personality. The secretive temper is to be
criticised; but it is not so fatal to character and dignity as its opposite. There
may be times when one must speak all
one's thought and emotion, — self is too
small to hold the joy or grief; but, having
done it, get back into your citadel of selfhood. We never quite respect the man
who tells us everything. Take your friends
into your heart, but not into your heart of
hearts; reserve that for yourself and duty.

(6.) Avoid absorbing and exclusive friendships. They are not wise; they are selfish,
and not of the nature of true friendship, —
forming a sort of common selfhood that is
but a double selfishness. They commonly
breed trouble, and end in quarrel and heart-
break.

This matter of friendship is often regarded slightingly, as a mere accessory of
life, a happy chance if one falls into it, but
not as entering into the substance of life

No mistake could be greater. It is not, as Emerson says, a thing of "glass threads or frost-work, but the solidest thing we know." "There is in friendship"—as Evelyn writes in the Life of Mrs. Godolphin—"something of all relations and something above them all. It is the golden thread that ties the hearts of all the world."

It is not pleasant to touch such a subject on its utilitarian side, still it is well to know that it is one of the largest factors of success not only in the social, but also in the commercial and political worlds. Many a merchant is carried through a crisis by his friends when the strict laws of business would have dropped him into ruin. It was Lincoln's immeasurable capacity for friendship that made his splendid career possible. It is this same superb quality that is preparing a like place in the hearts of the people for Garfield, — breaking out spontaneously in all his utterances, and vindicating its reality by an unmistakable ring. It is no idle thing. Happiness, success, character, destiny, largely turn upon it. I will know more of a man from knowing of his friendships, than I can gain from any other single source. Tell me if they are few or many, good or bad, warm or indifferent, and I will give you a reliable measure of the man.

Companionship logically goes before friendship, but I put it last, as the larger and more important relation for you to consider. One shapes itself by a law of affinity; the other is made. Choose your companions wisely, and your friendships will come about naturally.

Young men are often told that conceit and willfulness are their most marked qualities. I do not believe it. Their largest capability is that of inspiration. They do not readily take advice; they resent scolding, and utterly rebel against force, but they yield with the certainty of gravitation to personal influence. Through this capability all good and evil get into us. Youth is its period. Then heart and mind are open for all winds to blow through, — "airs from heaven or blasts from hell." A great part of the advantage of a college course is the contact for four years with a set of men who are scholars and gentlemen. It is impossible to overestimate the inspiring influence of contact with such men as President Woolsey, of Yale, and President Hopkins.

of Williams. "The strongest influence I took away from Yale," said an able graduate, "was the spirit of the president." "Something in President Hopkins's letter drew me to Williams," said Garfield. The healthiest influence at work to-day in English society — the most shaping in church and state — runs back to Dr. Arnold, of Rugby. He made the men that are now making England. Dean Stanley says of him, "His very presence seemed to create a new spring of health and vigor within them, and to give to life an interest and elevation which dwelt so habitually in their thoughts as a living image, that, when death had taken him away, the bond appeared to be still unbroken, and the sense of separation almost lost in the still deeper sense of a life and a union indestructible." It is often hard to tell where the good that is in us comes from, but most of it is inspired, — caught by contact with the good. "It is astonishing," says Mozley, "how much good goodness makes." Old John Brown said, "For a settler in a new country, one good believing man is worth a thousand without character." It is not the teaching of the pulpit or of the schools, but the men who walk up and down the streets, that determine the character of a community. If the leaders of society are not noble, no drill of teaching or pungency of exhortation will arouse high thoughts in the young.

I hesitate to touch the subject more closely, because it takes us into a field where it is nearly impossible to say anything that is not trite ; but if the subject does not admit of originality, it admits of earnestness. I ask you to look well to this matter of companions. Evil influences are not resistible. They may not always overcome, but they inevitably hurt.

For the sake of distinctness, let us put the matter into the form of rules.

Resolutely avoid all companionship that falls below your taste and standard of right. If it offends you, reject it with instant decision ; a second look is dangerous. Pope is now so little read that his wise lines may seem new : —

> " Vice is a monster of so frightful mien,
>   As, to be hated, needs but to be seen;
>   Yet seen too oft, familiar with her face,
>   We first endure, then pity, then embrace "

Familiarity with evil — the familiarity of contact or intimate knowledge — never ceases to be dangerous to any one. It is the glory and perfection of female virtue that it does not know evil. The Brooklyn preacher debauched his congregation when he preached on the sins of New York. The difficulty in securing an honest and decent police is due to their close contact with vice and crime. It is not in human nature to endure such contact and remain pure. Whenever you meet a person whose knowledge of evil ways is full and close and exact, you may be sure he is not sound at heart. Such knowledge is not knowledge, for knowledge pertains to order. A philosopher in chaos would have no vocation. If an associate swears, or lies, or drinks, or gambles; if he is tricky, or lascivious, or vile in his talk; if his thoughts easily run to baseness, put a wide space between him and yourself; give room for the pure winds of heaven to blow between you. But a closer distinction is to be made. Get at the temper of your associate; or, in your own sensible phrase, find out the kind of a fellow he is, before you make a friend of him. On the first show of meanness or lack of honor, let him go. If he is without a high ambition, beware of him. If his thoughts run strongly to one thing, — money, or dress, or society, or popularity, — he can do little for you. If he is cruel or negligent of duty to his family, if he is quick to take undue advantage, if he is penurious, if he scoffs at religion, if he derides the good, if he is skeptical of virtue, if he is scornful of good custom, you cannot afford to class yourself with him.

But one cannot always choose his associates. I do not forget how many of you are thrown together in the same office, or store, or shop, or mill, or class. But this does not necessitate intimate and sympathetic relations. Here is where you are to choose, and stand firm in your choice. The attitude of a mean or bad man is, Come to my level if you would be my friend; and he is right. Companionship must be on a level morally, though it need not be intellectually. An ignorant person may be a harmless and even pleasant friend. Sam Lawson, in Mrs. Stowe's "Oldtown Folks," was a very good companion for man or boy, despite his general good-for-nothingness. Men may associate, and waive almost all other differences but that of character. The moral line reaches up to heaven and down into eternal depths. It cannot be passed

and repassed. If you make companions of
the bad, you will end in being bad. "Live
with wolves," says the Spanish proverb,
"and you will learn to howl." It is the
beginning of a tragedy sad beyond thought
when a young man enters a set of a lower
moral tone than his own, — the set that
drinks a little, and gambles a little, and
discusses female frailty a little; some of
whom steal a little from their employers
on the score of a small salary, and drink a
little more than the rest on the ground of a
steadier head, and affect a little deeper
knowledge of the world, and lie with less
hesitation, and scoff with a louder accent:
it is not a pleasant sight to see a young
man cast by chance, or drawn by persua-
sion, into such a set as this. Superiority
of mind is not proof against it. It was the
wild smuggler boys of Kirkoswald who led
Burns astray.

It is one of the worst features of modern
society that such sets as these are everywhere taking an actual organization — mem-
bership and rooms and fees. Society, from
top to bottom, is running to clubs. It is
a matter not easily disposed of, — having a
good and a bad side. In a complex state
of society, such forms of social life will be

created. But when the clubs are organized on a basis of drink and cards and " a good time generally," there is little question as to their influence. They destroy more than moral principles ; they wreck manhood and health and high purpose and self-respect. A young man may enter such a club, but no man comes out of it. Manhood evaporates under this organized pressure of inanity and vice, and leaves something fitter to creep than to walk, — " beastly transformations," who

"Nor once perceive their foul disfigurement,
But boast themselves more comely than before."

But let us get over to the positive and better side of our subject. I make as a last suggestion that you associate as much as possible with persons of true worth and nobility of character. The main use of a great man is to inspire others. There is a truth parallel to the doctrine of Apostolic Succession by the laying on of hands, which, to my mind, is better than the doctrine. The succession of all high and noble life is through personality. Seek always the superior man. If you are already in a calling, get amongst those who excel in it. Every professional man will tell you that he cannot meet one of low grade in his calling without injury, nor one high up without fresh stimulus. It is well to get near men of reputed energy and worth. The fascination that draws us to the great is deep and divine; it is a call to share their greatness, — the divine way of distributing it to all. Get close to men of energy, and see how they work, — to men of thought, and catch their spirit and method; get near the refined and cultivated in mind and manners, and feel their charm. The influence nearest that of Omnipotence upon a young man is that of a noble, intelligent, refined woman; not one who may become his wife, but one older and out of all such question. The friendship of such a woman, Steele says, is equal to a liberal education.

But if you are cut off from this world of inspiring influence, if those about you are dry and dull and commonplace, seek the companionship you need in books: fellowship with the great spirits of history; dream with the poets; think with the philosophers; exult with martyrs; triumph with heroes; overcome with saints. Indeed, books are among the best of companions; but of that hereafter.

III.

MANNERS.

"High thoughts seated in a heart of courtesy." — SIDNEY.

"The compliments and ceremonies of our breeding should recall, however remotely, the grandeur of our destiny." — EMERSON.

"Love as brethren, be pitiful, be courteous." — ST. PAUL

"Who misses or who wins the prize?
Go, lose or conquer as you can;
But if you fail, or if you rise,
Be each, pray God, a gentleman."
Epilogue to Dr. Birch and his Pupils.

III.

MANNERS.

PERHAPS there is no better starting-point in this subject than the one most remote from its real centre, — our national manners. The foreign critics tell us that we are rapidly improving in our behavior; we are too conscious of the need to resent the patronizing comment, and silently wait for the sure coming of that type of manners — higher than has yet been realized — when our institutions have fully ripened the character of the people.

In the externals of behavior we are in advance of the last generation. The immense development in taste and art that has come about through foreign travel and world-expositions has a correspondence in manners. Uncouthness of dress, roughness of speech, and the general barbarity of manners that prevailed in large sections of the country have largely passed away. The salutations, respect for another's personality, the care of the person, the tones of the voice, and the use of language, — all are better than they were. Is there also an improvement of feeling and mutual relation? The external, in the main, is indicative of what is within. Great masses of people are not hypocrites. The kindlier address shows a kinder and more equal spirit. The deference of a century ago was the offspring of aristocracy; that, indeed, has passed away with the dying out of its source. But if we no longer bow down before our fellows, we entertain for them a truer and more rational respect. To go a little closer into the matter, the masses have greatly improved in manners, but the class that used to be regarded as aristocratic and specially well-bred has deteriorated, as was to be expected. The withdrawal of the deference of the lower classes, as our institutions began to be felt, threw them into confusion. The old-time aristocrat — and a very noble figure he was — is consciously out of place and relations; his manners suffer in consequence, and now, like Portia's English suitor, he " gets his behavior everywhere."

But we must not infer that we are yet a people of refined manners. Dr. Bushnell, forty years ago, said that emigration tended to barbarism. We are a nation of emigrants ; the greater part of us, for two hundred years, have lived in the woods, and the shadows of primeval forests still overhang us. There must be more intelligence, more culture, a more evenly distributed wealth, a denser population, and a fuller realization of our national idea, which is also the Christian idea, — personality, — before we can claim to be a well-bred people. In Europe, the good manners of the great percolate down to the masses. One consequently hears and sees there a delicacy of behavior and gentleness of address not common here. It is, however, largely external and a matter of imitation. We have few such outstanding examples, and whatever of attainment we have is genuine and from within. We are destined to see on this continent a form of manners more genuinely refined and noble than the world has yet known. Just now we are in an open place between the going out of aristocratic or feudal habits and ways and the coming in of a culture and behavior based

on equality and mutual respect. It must
be confessed that we are without great con-
spicuous examples of the kind of gentleman
that is to be looked for in this country.
Washington was undoubtedly a very true
and noble gentleman ; but he was not the
American gentleman of the future, being
essentially English. With certain abate-
ments and additions in minor respects, Lincoln must be regarded as coming nearer our
true type. A President who called to his
cabinet a man who had publicly insulted
him by use of the most opprobrious epithet
the language offers, and appointed to the
chief-justiceship another who spoke of him
with habitual contempt, showed qualities of
character that we find in no other great
American.

But let us get nearer our subject. Every
young man desires above all else to be regarded as a gentleman. None of us can
bear any other imputation. You may ac-
cuse one of violating the entire decalogue
with less offense than if you tell him he is
not a gentleman. Here is something very
deep and weighty. What is this that so
outweighs every other good word and estimate ? So fine a thing necessarily has

many counterfeits; and so we will search it with definitions.

The word undoubtedly comes from the Latin *gens*, meaning tribe or family. Hence all the one-sided and incomplete notions that a gentleman is a man of family. It is a good thing to be well born, with inherited tastes and traditions; but birth does not make the gentleman. It is unfortunate that, etymologically, the word does not come from *gentle* and *man*. The world would have been better if it had entertained such a conception of the highest type of man, for the epithet nearly covers the whole of the character. Julius Hare, himself a fine illustration of his definition, says: "A gentleman should be gentle in everything; at least in everything that depends upon himself,—in carriage, temper, construction, aims, desires. He ought, therefore, to be mild, calm, quiet, temperate; not hasty in judgment, not exorbitant in ambition, not overbearing, not proud, not rapacious, not oppressive." Ruskin makes the leading traits of a gentleman to be fineness, sensitiveness, and sympathy, each involving the other. Professor Lieber, who has written on the subject in a manly way,

says: " The word gentleman signifies that
character which is distinguished by strict
honor, self-possession, forbearance, generous
as well as refined feelings, and polished de-
portment, — a character to which all meanness, explosive irritability, and peevish fret-
fulness are alien ; to which, consequently, a
generous candor, scrupulous veracity and
essential truthfulness, courage, both moral
and physical, dignity and self-respect, liber-
ality in thought, argument, and conduct are
habitual, and have become natural. It implies also refinement of feelings and lofti-
ness of conduct to the dictates of morality
and the precepts of religion, — a long, hard
sentence, but well worth our study." Mr.
Calvert says: " The gentleman is never unduly familiar ; takes no liberties ; is chary
of questions ; is neither artificial nor af-
fected ; is as little obtrusive upon the mind
or feelings of others as on their persons ;
bears himself tenderly towards the weak
and unprotected ; is not arrogant ; cannot
be supercilious ; can be self-denying without
struggle ; is not vain of his advantages, ex-
trinsic personal ; habitually subordinates
his lower to his higher self ; is, in his best
condition, electric with truth, buoyant with

veracity." Mr. Emerson, who writes on the theme with keenest inward sympathy, as well as discrimination, says: " The gentleman is a man of truth, lord of his own actions, and expressing that lordship in his behavior; not in any manner dependent and servile either on persons, or opinions, or possessions. Beyond this fact of truth and real force, the word denotes good nature or benevolence, — manhood first, and then gentleness." Sir Philip Sidney — himself the ideal gentleman — put the whole matter into one pregnant phrase: " High thoughts seated in a heart of courtesy." You will notice that in the conception of a gentleman which these authors give the moral element predominates; not family, or station, or manners, but qualities. They do, indeed, take on and draw after them external forms, for the *in* and the *out* must at last be alike ; but the essential condition, that which makes one a gentleman, is moral qualities.

Following this unanimous hint, we will try to get these qualities into some order. We name, —

1. Truth. One who well knew described a perfect man as one who "speaketh the

truth in his heart," — inward truthfulness, outward veracity; this goes before all else in making up the gentleman. Calvert says: "A gentleman may brush his own shoes or clothes, or mend or make them, or roughen his hands with the helve, or foul them with dye-work or iron-work; but he must not foul his mouth with a lie." A lie makes relations impossible. When two persons meet, there can be no true conversation unless it is thoroughly understood that each is himself: I am I, and you are you; I say what is true, and I believe that you say what is true. This is the foundation of all human intercourse. Nor can a man long be himself who does not speak the truth. He duplicates and reduplicates himself, loses all sense of personality, and becomes a mere phenomenon, flickering amongst men with a false light, trusted by none, and at last is lost even to himself; for a liar finally ceases to believe himself; his memory, judgment, and even senses fail to bring him true reports. There is no girdle that will hold a man together and make him a person but the truth. And so it enters fundamentally into the highest type of personal character. Amongst those who wear the title of gentleman, it takes precedence of all else, even kingly dignity. Charles I. said to the Commoners, "You have not only the word of a king, but of a gentleman." When Nicholas of Russia desired to assure the English ambassador that he was speaking the truth, he said, "I desire to speak with you as a gentleman." The reason that some occupations traditionally exclude those following them from the rank of gentlemen is because they foster lying. In certain forms of trade, where the values are unknown, or variable, or obscure, the temptation to lie is so strong that it becomes nearly universal, and those following such callings are presumed to be unworthy of the society of gentlemen. Truthfulness is the chastity of men ; when once sacrificed, caste is forever lost. A gentleman not only speaks the truth, but is truthful. " He never dodges," says Emerson. He looks squarely at person or thing, because he proposes to see things and persons as they are. And being attuned to truth within, his voice will have the pitch of truth ; the very poise of his body and sway of his members will have a certain directness born of truth. We name, —

2. Kindness of heart, — "The willing-

ness and faculty to oblige," Emerson calls
it.   If one have not this, he may step aside.
If truth is the foundation of good manners,
kindness is the superstructure, — that which
most appears and constitutes them.   The
phraseology of refined society is expressive
of love and interest.   We begin letters with
a term of endearment, and we used to end
them with an assurance of humble service.
Those were fine old every-day words, — now
used too little, — " I am at your service,"
" What are your commands ? "   The gentleman exists to help ; he has no other vocation.   If you desire to cultivate yourselves
in this matter, let your husbandry be in this
direction.   A spirit of universal good-will,
a generous heart, and an open hand, — be
strong in these, and you may claim this
badge of highest nobility.   But if you are
exclusive, if you lack heart, if your hand is
kept closed except when pried open by
shame or stout appeal, if you go about in a
spirit of caution and reserve and secret dis-
dain of all but your set, you are out of our
high category ; neither money, birth, nor
sleekness can smuggle you in.   The immense
mistake in this matter is that the tokens of
good-will are made partial and exclusive

There are enough to love and help their own, but such consideration gives no true title to the rank of gentleman. It is the very essence of gentlemanhood that one is helpful to the weak, the poor, the friend-less, the humble, the miserable, the de-graded. A gentleman will not be too cau-tious where he bestows his favors. The economists preach against street beggars, but your Charles Lamb cannot be kept from dropping frequent pennies into their hats. He is not too critical of the testi-monials of the shipwrecked sailor, and he sees the wan face and rags of poverty more than he listens to its improbable tale. He does not mind whose bundle he carries, if so he relieves some aching arm; nor how low the door-way he enters, if he can carry cheer across the threshold.

(3.) If truth is the foundation and kind-ness is the superstructure of the gentleman, *honor* is his atmosphere, — a hard thing to define, but a very real thing as we see it, or the lack of it. It is akin to truth, but is more, — its aroma, its flower, its soul. It is that which makes a gentleman's word as good as his bond. We get its exact mean-ing when it is used in connection with fe-

male virtue. It may be defined as an exquisite and imperative self-respect. Honor is
an absolute and ultimate thing. It knows
nothing of abatement, or change, or degree.
It governs with a noble and inexorable necessity. The man of honor dies sooner than
break its lightest behest. To those who do
not know it it is less than the summer
cloud; to those who have it adamant is not
so solid. The man of honor may be trusted
to the uttermost; he does not know temptation. It is a mail that prevents even the
aiming of arrows. Charles Sumner thought
there was but little bribery in Washington;
he had never seen anything of it. The
man of honor has no price. Mr. Smiles, in
one of his admirable books, says that Wel-
lington was once offered half a million for a
state secret not of any special value to the
government, but the keeping of which was
a matter of honor. " It appears you are capable of keeping a secret," he said to the
official. "Certainly," he replied. "Then so
am I," said the general, and bowed him out.
Honor is offended even at the thought of
its violation. It is the poetry of noble man
hood, —

> " That away,
> Men are but gilded loam or painted clay."

Unhappy is he who comes to years of manhood and finds it weak and dull; unhappier still is he who has lost it by some deliberate act. He can never again be quite the same man. Tarnished honor in man or woman is the one stain that cannot be washed out. The best word upon it in all literature, I think, is in that fine poem of Burns's, " Epistle to a Young Friend : " —

> " But where ye feel your honor grip,
>   Let that aye be your border;
>   Its slightest touches, instant pause;
>   Debar a' side pretences,
>   And resolutely keep its laws,
>   Uncaring consequences."

(4.) We put next *delicacy*, — fineness of fibre. It is made up of quick perception and fine feeling. It leads one to see instantly the line beyond which he may not go; to detect the boundary between friendliness and familiarity, between earnestness and heat, between sincerity and intolerance in pressing your convictions, between style and fussiness, between deference and its excess. It is the critic and mentor of the gentlemanly character. It tells him what is coarse and unseemly and rude and excessive. It warns him away from all doubtful acts and persons. It gives little or no reason, — it is too fine for analysis and logical process, — but acts like a divine instinct, and is to be heeded as divine. A man may be good without it, but he will lack a nameless grace; he will fail of highest respect; he will miss the best companionship; he will make blunders that hurt him without his knowing why; he will feel a reproach that he cannot understand. It is this quality more than any other that draws the line in all rational society. Men often wonder why they are shut out of certain grades of society; they are well dressed, intelligent, moral, rich, amiable, — still the door is shut. Let them, if they can, measure their *fibre*, and they will usually get at the cause. It is this quality that decides matters of dress, the length and frequency of visits; that discriminates between the shadow and substance in all matters of etiquette. It determines the nature and number of questions one may ask of another, and sees everywhere and always the invisible boundary that invests personality.

(5.) I name next *respect and consideration for others*, — something more than kindness and less ethereal than delicacy, but entering quite as largely and imperatively

into the every-day life of the gentleman.
You perceive at once that it is of the very
nature of our faith, — not self, but another.
To consider tenderly the feelings, opinions,
circumstances, of others, — what is this but
Christian ?

There is one respect in which our Anglo-Saxon race — especially when the Norman strain is thin — is simply brutal in its
manners, namely, its treatment of the ludicrous when it involves pain. A person,
old or young, on sitting down, misses the
chair and comes to the floor, and the room
screams with laughter. What could be more
essentially cruel and barbarous ? A public
speaker stammers, and the audience giggles.
They would be kinder, he thinks, if they
would pelt him with the foot-stools. A
mistake, a peculiarity, an accident, often
involves a ludicrous element, but it is well
to remember that a sense of the ludicrous
is not the loftiest of emotions. The simple
question in such cases is not, How does the
looker-on feel ? but, How does the other person feel ? If there were a litany of good
manners, it might well begin, From giggling, good Lord, deliver us. The word
vulgar will not often be found on these

pages, but we would like to gather up all
the meaning and emphasis lodged in it
and pour them upon this habit of inconsid-
erate laughter at the misfortunes of others.

Let us hasten to the pleasanter side of our
subject. The great historical illustration
of this grace of consideration, never to be
passed by, is that of Sidney, at the battle
of Zutphen, handing the cup of water, for
which he longed with dying thirst, to the
wounded soldier beside him : " He needs it
more than I."

"How far that little candle throws his beams !"

Like it is the incident of Sir Ralph Ab-
ercrombie, — told by Smiles, — who, when
mortally wounded, found under his head the
blanket of a private soldier, placed there
to ease his dying pains. " Whose blanket
is this ? " " Duncan Roy's." " See that
Duncan Roy gets his blanket this very
night," said Sir Ralph, and died without
its comfort. Smiles gives another fine in-
stance of this divine grace, all the better
from its spontaneity. Two English nav-
vies in Paris saw, one rainy day, a hearse,
with its burden, winding along the streets,
unattended by a single mourner. Falling

in behind, they followed it to the ceme-
tery. It was only sentiment, but it was
fine and true. Such sentiment leads a captain to go down with his ship; the fire-
man to pass through flame; the soldier to
go on the forlorn hope. When spontaneous,
it shows that our nature is sound at the
core; when wrought into a conscious habit
it reveals the divine glory that every life
may take on.

One imbued with this high quality never
sees personal deformity or blemish. A lame
man could easily classify his friends as to
their breeding by drawing a line between
those who ask *how it happened* and those
who refrain from all question. I say dis
tinctly, the gentleman never *sees* deform
ity. He will not talk to a beggar of his
rags, nor boast of his health before the sick,
nor speak of his wealth amongst the poor;
he will not seem to be fortunate amongst
the hapless, nor make any show of his virtue before the vicious. He will avoid all
painful contrast, always looking at the thing
in question from the stand-point of the other
person.

The gentleman is largely dowered with
forbearance. The preacher will not dog-

matize nor indulge in personality since his
audience has no chance to reply. The lawyer will not browbeat the witness — no, not
even to win his case — if he is a gentleman.
The physician is as delicate as purity itself,
and as secretive as the grave. There is no
finer touch-stone of the gentleman than
the forbearing use of power or advantage
over another: the employer to his men, the
husband to his wife, the creditor to his
debtor, the rich to the poor, the educated
to the ignorant, the teacher to pupils, the
prosperous to the unfortunate.

> " Oh, it is excellent
> To have a giant's strength ; but it is tyrannous
> To use it like a giant."

(6.) How far are manners to be made a
matter of rule? is a question you will inevitably ask. *From within out* — is the fundamental law in manners ; still there is an
external view of the subject quite worth
heeding.

There is a certain fine robustness of character that is prone to pay little heed to the
" thou shalt " and " thou shalt not " of society ; and there is a certain spirituality
that says, " Make your own rules." There
is much truth in both positions, but it is

delicate ground to tread on; one needs to be very sure-footed and quick-eyed to avoid falls. Upon the whole, and for the most of us, it is better there should be a code of social laws, well understood and rather carefully observed; at least, one should always have them at hand, ready for use. There are many things that help to make life easy and agreeable that are not taught by intuition. Nor could we live together in mutual convenience unless we agreed upon certain arbitrary rules as to daily intercourse. If it is well to have these common habits and interchanges of courtesy, it is well to have them in the best form, even to punctiliousness. Without doubt, what are called *the manners of society* are not only a part of gentlemanhood, but are extremely convenient. I am not about to indicate these rules, but I may suggest that in all matters of dress, of care of the person, of carriage, of command of the features and voice and eyes, and of what are called the ways of good society, it is of great use to be well informed. They will not take you one step on the way, but they will smooth it, and the lack of them may block it altogether. The main dependence must be on the things we have considered. If one is centrally true, kind, honorable, delicate, and considerate, he will almost without fail have manners that will take him into any circle where culture and taste prevail over folly. Still, this inward seed needs training. It should levy on all graceful forms, on practice and discipline, on observation, on fashion even, and make them subserve its native grace. Watch those of excellent reputation in manners. Keep your eyes open when you go to the metropolis, and learn its grace; or, if you live in the city, when you go to the country, mark the higher quality of simplicity. Catch the temper of the great masters of literature: the nobility of Scott, the sincerity of Thackeray, the heartiness of Dickens, the tenderness of MacDonald, the delicacy of Tennyson, the grace of Longfellow, the repose of Shakespeare.

Manners in this high sense, and so learned, take one far on in the world. They are irresistible. If you meet the king he will recognize you as a brother. They are a defense against insult. All doors fly open when he who wears them approaches. They cannot be bought. They cannot be learned as from a book they cannot pass from lip to lip ; they come from within, and from a *within* that is grounded in truth, honor, delicacy, kindness, and consideration.

These pages may fall under the eyes of some readers along with the Christmas-tide. No theme is more appropriate to it. The spirit of these days is alive with tenderest courtesy. A gentleman can have no better watchword than that sung at Bethlehem: " Peace on earth, good-will to men."

> " Come wealth or want, come good or ill,
>   Let old and young accept their part,
> And bow before the awful will,
>   And bear it with an honest heart.
>
> " Who misses or who wins the prize ?
>   Go, lose or conquer as you can ;
> But if you fail, or if you rise,
>   Be each, pray God, a gentleman.
>
> " A gentleman, or old or young !
>   (Bear kindly with my humble lay.)
> The sacred chorus first was sung
>   Upon the first of Christmas days ;
>
> " The shepherds heard it overhead,
>   The joyful angels raised it then:
> Glory to God on high, it said,
>   And peace on earth to gentle — men." [1]

[1] Epilogue to *Dr. Birch and his Young Friends.*

IV.

THRIFT.

Economy, whether public or private, means the wise management of labor; and it means it mainly in three senses: namely, first, *applying* your labor rationally; secondly, *preserving* its produce carefully; lastly, *distributing* its produce seasonably." — RUSKIN.

" In the morning sow thy seed, and in the evening withhold not thy hand; for thou knowest not whether shall prosper, either this or that, or whether they shall be alike good." — SOLOMON.

" The virtues are economists." — EMERSON.

" No man can guage the value, at this present critical time, of a steady stream of young men, flowing into all professions and all industries, who have learned resolutely to speak in a society such as ours : 'I can't afford.' " — THOMAS HUGHES.

IV.

THRIFT.

WE have so long been told that we are a thrifty people that we go on assuming it as a fact without fresh examination. Thrift is more apt to be a phase than a characteristic of the life of a nation, — a habit than a principle. That we are thrifty because our ancestors were no more follows than that the ship that sails out of the harbor stanch and tight will be sound when she returns from a long and stormy voyage. It was not from any instinct or natural trait that our forefathers were thrifty, but from a moral necessity. The Celt is naturally thrifty. The Anglo-Saxon is thrifty only when there is some strong motive behind or before him; he is thrifty for a reason; and this certainly is the best foundation of the virtue. The early settlers found themselves here in circumstances out of keeping with their characters, — rich in one and poor in the other, and so set about overcoming the discrepancy. Their large and noble conceptions of man required that he should be well housed and cared for. Dr. Holmes says: " I never saw a house too fine to shelter the human head. Elegance fits man." When Nero built his palace of marble and ivory and gold, he said, " This is a fit house for a man." The scientists tell us that environment and life stand in a relation of necessity; they certainly stand in the relation of fitness. The strong, divinely nourished common sense of our fathers perceived this, and they husbanded as earnestly as they prayed. They could give up all for a cause, and take no thought for the morrow, if the occasion required, but they knew how to discriminate between the rare occasion of total self-sacrifice and the conduct of every-day life. Consequently thrift early got a strong hold. New England has had two great inspiring minds, — Jonathan Edwards and Benjamin Franklin. Far apart in spirit and character, they formed a grand unity in their influence. One taught religion, the other thrift; one clarified theology, the other taught the people how to get on. Edwards tided New England over the infidelity that

prevailed in the last century; Franklin
created the wealth that feeds society to-day
by inspiring a passion for thrift. Hence,
for a century, irreligion and beggary were
equally a reproach, and still in no country
in the world is the latter held so vile.

But these two formative influences are
evidently waning. Nor is it to be altogether
regretted. Both were too austere to be per-
petually healthful; neither regarded the
breadth and scope of human nature. The
danger is lest the ebb be excessive, and its
method be exchanged for others not so sure
and wholesome. Thrift pertains to details.
It is alike our glory and our fault that we
are impatient of details. Our courage
prompts to risks, our large-mindedness in-
vites to great undertakings; both somewhat adverse to thrift, — one essentially,
and the other practically, — because great
undertakings are for the few, while thrift
is for all. Large enterprises make the few
rich, but the majority prosper only through
the carefulness and detail of thrift. To
speak of it is a Scylla and Charybdis voyage, — while shunning the jaws of waste,
there is danger of drifting upon the rocks
of meanness. I say frankly, if either fate

is to befall us, I would rather it were not the last.

I begin by insisting on the importance of having money. Speculate and preach about it as we will, the great factor in society is money. As the universe of worlds needs some common force like gravitation to hold them together and keep them apart, so society requires some dominating passion or purpose to hold its members in mutual relations. Money answers this end. Without some such general purpose or passion, society would be chaotic; men could not work together, could achieve no common results, could have no common standards of virtue and attainment. Bulwer says: "Never treat money affairs with levity; money is character." And indeed character for the most part is determined by one's relation to money. Find out how one gets, saves, spends, gives, lends, borrows, and bequeathes money, and you have the character of the man in full outline. "If one does all these wisely," says Henry Taylor, "it would almost argue a perfect man." Nearly all the virtues play about the use of money, — honesty, justice, generosity, charity, frugality, forethought, self sacrifice. The poor man is called to certain great and strenuous virtues, but he has not the full field of conduct open to him as it is to the man of wealth. He may undergo a very deep and valuable discipline, but he will not get the full training that a rich man may. St. Paul compassed the matter in knowing how to *abound* as well as how to suffer want. Poverty is a limitation all the way through; it is good only as in all evil there is "a soul of goodness." Mr. Jarvis says, " Among the poor there is less vital force, a lower tone of life, more ill health, more weakness, more early death." If poverty is our lot, we must bear it bravely, and contend against its chilling and stifling influences; but we are not to think of it as good, or in any way except as something to be avoided or gotten rid of, if honor and honesty permit it. I wish I could fill every young man who reads these pages with an utter dread and horror of poverty. I wish I could make you so feel its shame, its constraint, its bitterness, that you would make vows against it. You would then read patiently what I shall say of thrift. You may already have a sufficiently ill opinion of poverty, but you may not un-

6

derstand that one is already poverty-stricken if his habits are not thrifty. Every day I see young men — well dressed, with full purses and something of inheritance await- ing them — as plainly foredoomed to pov- erty as if its rags hung about them.

The secret of thrift is forethought. Its process is saving for use; it involves also judicious spending. The thrifty man saves: savings require investments in stable and remunerative forms; hence that order and condition of things that we call civilization, which does not exist until one generation passes on the results of its labors and sav- ings to the next. Thus thrift underlies civilization as well as personal prosperity. The moment it ceases to act society ret- rogrades towards savagery, the main feat- ure of which is absence of forethought. A spendthrift or idler is essentially a savage: a generation of them would throw society back into barbarism. There is a large num- ber of young men — chiefly to be found in cities — who rise from their beds at eleven or twelve; breakfast in a club-house; idle away the afternoon in walking or driving; spend a part of the evening with their fam- ilies, the rest at some place of amusement or in meeting the engagements of society, bringing up at the club-house or some gambling den or place of worse repute; and early in the morning betake themselves to bed again. They do no work; they read but little; they have no religion; they are as a class vicious. I depict them simply to classify them. These men are essentially savages. Except in some slight matters of taste and custom, they are precisely the individuals Stanley found in Central Africa, with some advantages in favor of the African. Some years ago, Mr. Buckle startled the reading world by putting the Roman Catholics of Spain and the high Calvinists of Scotland in the same class, as alike in the generic trait of bigotry, though differing in matters of belief. Precisely in the same way, and with the same logical correctness, these idlers are to be put in the same category with savages. They live under the fundamental characteristic of savagery, namely, improvidence. Our young man of leisure has a rich father, and the African has his perennial banana, and, upon the whole, rather a surer outlook.

The chief distinction between civilization and barbarism turns on thrift. Thrift

is the builder of society.   Thrift redeems
man from savagery.

What are its methods?

(1.) I name the first in one word, — *save.*
Thrift has no rule so imperative and without exception.   If you have an allowance,
teach yourself on no account to exhaust it.
The margin between income and expenditure is sacred ground, and must not be
touched except for weightiest reasons.   But
if you are earning a salary, — it matters
not how small, — plan to save some part of
it.   If you receive seventy-five cents per
day, live on seventy; if one dollar, spend
but ninety; you save thirty dollars a year,
— enough to put you into the category of
civilization.   But he who spends all must
not complain if we set him down logically
a savage.   Your saving is but little, but it
represents a feeling and a purpose, and,
small as it is, it divides a true from a spu-
rious manhood.

Life in its last analysis is a struggle.
The main question for us all is, Which is
getting the advantage, self or the world?
When one is simply holding his own,
spending all he earns, and has nothing between himself and this " rough world," he

in a fair way to be worsted in the battle.
He inevitably grows weaker, while the piti-
less world keeps to its pitch of heavy exac-
tion.

There is a sense of strength and advantage springing from however slight gains
essential to manly character. Say what
we will about "honest poverty," — and I
would say nothing against it, for I well
know that God may build barriers of poverty about a man, not to be passed, yet
within which he may nourish a royal manhood, — still the men who escape from poverty into independence wear a nobler mien
than those who keep even with the world.
Burns is the poet of the poor man, and has
almost glorified poverty, but he never put
into any of his verses more of his broad
common sense than into these : —

> "To catch Dame Fortune's golden smile,
>   Assiduous wait upon her;
> And gather gear by ev'ry wile
>   That 's justified by honor:
> Not for to hide it in a hedge,
>   Nor for a train attendant;
> But for the glorious privilege
>   Of being independent."

It is a great part of this battle of life to
keep a good heart. The prevailing mood
of the poor is that of sadness. Their gayety

is forced and fitful. Their drinking habits are the cause and result of their poverty. There is no repose, no sense of adequacy, no freedom, after one has waked up to the fact that he is poor. It takes but little to redeem one from this feeling. The spirit and purpose of saving thrift change the whole color of life. It is not necessary to have already made accumulations to secure your own or others' indorsement of your manliness. The direction you face will be sufficient. I recall the homely story of the young man who applied to the father of "the dearest girl in the world" for permission to marry, and, in answer to the searching and inevitable question (don't forget that you must meet it) as to his resources and ability to support a wife, was obliged to confess that he had no money, but declared that he was " chock-full of day's work." Money was only a question of time.

It can hardly be expected that you will look ahead twenty or forty years, and realize the actual stings of poverty and the sharper stings of thriftless habits; but it may be expected that you will see why it is wiser and more manly to save than to spend.

There is a certain fascinating glare about the young man who spends freely; whose purse is always open, whether deep or shallow; who is always ready to foot the bills; who says *yes* to every proposal, and produces the money. I have known such in the past, but as I meet them now I find them quite as ready to foot the bills, but generally unable to do so. I have noticed also that the givers, and the benefactors of society, had no such youthhood. This popular and fascinating young man is in reality a very poor creature; very interesting he may be in the matter of drinks, and billiards, and theatre tickets, and sleigh-rides, and clothes, and club-rates; but when he earns five or eight or ten hundred dollars a year, and spends it chiefly in this way, would charity itself call him anything but a fool? The boys hail him a royal good fellow, and the girls pet him, but who respects him? I do not write of him here with any hope of bettering him; he is of the class of whom it is said that an experience in a mortar would be a failure. I speak to a higher grade of intelligence. The painful fact, however, is to be recognized, that the saving habit is losing ground. The reasons are evident : city and country are one. The standards of dress, amusements, and life generally are set in the richer circles of the metropolis, and are observed, at whatever cost, in all other circles. I can do nothing to offset these influences but to remind you of nobler methods. I can only say that to spend all one earns is a mistake ; that while to spend, except in a severe and judicious way, weakens character, economy dignifies and strengthens it.

The habit of saving is itself an education. It fosters every virtue. It teaches self-denial. It cultivates a sense of order. It trains to forethought, and so broadens the mind. It reveals the meaning of the word *business*, which is something very different from its routine. One may know all the forms of business, even in a practical way, without having the business characteristic. Were a merchant to choose for a partner a young man thoroughly conversant with the business, but having expensive, self-indulgent personal habits, or one not yet versed in its details, but who knows how to keep a dollar when he has earned it, he would unhesitatingly take the latter. The habit of saving, while it has its dangers, even fosters generosity. The great givers have been great savers. The miserly habit is not acquired, but is inborn. Not there lies the danger. The divinely-ordered method of saving so educates and establishes such order in the man, and brings him into so intelligent a relation to the world, that he becomes a benefactor. It is coarse thinking to confound spending with generosity, or saving with meanness.

(2.) I vary the strain but little when I say, Avoid a self-indulgent spending of money.

The great body of young men in our country are in the receipt of such incomes that the question whether a thing can be afforded or not becomes a highly rational inquiry. With incomes ranging from a dollar or less per day to a thousand dollars a year, there is room for the play of that wise word, *afford*. I think it tends to shut out several things that are very generally indulged in. I have no intention of saying anything here against the pleasant habit of smoking, except to set it in the light of this common-sense word, *afford*. Your average salaries are, say, five hundred dollars. If you smoke cigars, your smallest daily allow-

ance will be two, costing at least twenty
cents, — I assume that you do not degrade
yourselves by using the five-cent article, —
more than seventy dollars a year. If it were
fifty, it would be a tenth of your salary.
The naked question for a rational being to
consider is, Can I afford to spend a tenth
or seventh of my income in a mere indulgence? What has common sense to say to
the proportion? Would not this amount,
lodged in some sound investment, contribute rather more to self-respect? Ten years
of such expenditure represent probably a
thousand dollars, for there is an inevitable
ratio of increase in all self-indulgent habits;
fifty years represent five thousand, — more
than most men will have at sixty-five, who
began life with so poor an understanding of
the word *afford*. Double these estimates,
and they will be all the truer. I do not
propose in these pages to enter on a crusade
against tobacco, but I may remind you that
the eye of the world is fixed on the tobacco
habit with a very close gaze. The educators
in Europe and America are agreed that it
impairs mental energy. Life-insurance companies are shy of its peculiar pulse. Ocu-
lists say that it weakens the eyes. Physi

cians declare it to be a prolific cause of
dyspepsia, and hence of other ills. The
vital statistician finds in it an enemy of vir
ility. It is asserted by the leading authori-
ties in each department that it takes the
spring out of the nerves, the firmness out of
the muscles, the ring out of the voice ; that
it renders the memory less retentive, the
judgment less accurate, the conscience less
quick, the sensibilities less acute ; that it
relaxes the will, and dulls every faculty of
body and mind and moral nature, dropping
the entire man down in the scale of his powers, and so is to be regarded as one of the
wasters of society. I do not undertake to
affirm all these propositions, but only to
show how the social critics of the day are
regarding the subject.

The habit of drinking is so nearly parallel with smoking in its relation to thrift
that it need not detain us. The same co-
gent word *afford* applies here with stronger
emphasis, because the drinking habit involves a larger ratio of increase. Waiving
any moral considerations involved in beer
drinking, the fact of its *cost* should throw it
out. The same startling figures we have
used are more than true here. It is not a

thrifty habit, and no young man who has his way to make in the world is entitled to an unthrifty habit. It is idle to repeat the truisms of the theme. We have heard till we cease to heed that drink is the great waster of society. Great Britain spends annually two hundred and fifty millions of dollars in drink. Our own statistics are nearly as bad. It is the one thing — even if it does not reach the proportions of a vice — that keeps more men out of a competence than all other causes combined. The twin habits of smoking and beer-drinking stand for a respectable property to all who indulge in them, — a thing the greater part will never have, though they have had it. " The Gods sell all things at a fair price," says the proverb; but they sell nothing dearer than these two indulgences, since the price is commonly the man himself.

The simple conclusion that common sense forces upon us is that a young man fronting life cannot *afford* to drink; he cannot afford the money; he cannot afford to bear the reputation, nor run the risks it involves.

I refer next to the habit of light and foolish spending. Emerson says, " The farmer's dollar is heavy; the clerk's is light and nimble, leaps out of his pockets, jumps on to cards and faro tables." But it gets into no more foolish place than the till of the showman, and minstrel troupe, and theatrical company. I do not say these things are bad. When decent, they are allowable as an occasional recreation, but here, as before, the sense of proportion must be observed ; not what I like, but what I can *afford.*

It has been said that no one should carry coin loose in the pocket, as too easily got at. I would vary it by applying the Spanish proverb, " Before forty, nothing ; after forty, anything." If one has been careful in early life he may be careless after. At first let the purse be stout and well tied with stout strings ; later there need be no purse, but only an open hand.

It seems to be an excess of simplicity to suggest that a young man should purchase nothing that he does not actually want, nothing because it is cheap ; to resist the glittering appeals of jewels and gay clothing and delicate surroundings. These will come in due order.

(3.) It is an essential condition of thrift that one should keep to legitimate occupations. There is no thrift in chance; its central idea is *order*, — a series of causes and effects along the line of which fore-thought can look and make its calculations. Speculation makes the few rich and the many poor. Thrift divides the prizes of life to those who deserve them. If the great fortunes are the results of specula-tions, the average competencies have their foundation and permanence in thrifty ways.

(4.) Have a thorough knowledge of your affairs ; leave nothing at loose ends; be ex-act in every business transaction. The chief source of quarrel in the business world is what is termed " an understand-ing," ending commonly in a misunderstand-ing. It is not ungenerous or ignoble al-ways to insist on a full, straight-out bar-gain, and it falls in with the thrifty habit.

It is a very simple matter to name, but the habit of keeping a strict account of per-sonal expenses down to the penny has great educational power. Keep such a book, tab-ulate its items at the close of the year, — so much for necessaries, so much for luxuries, so much for worse than luxuries, — and isten to what it reports to you.

(5.) Debt is the secret foe of thrift, as

vice and idleness are its open foes. It may
sometimes be wise for one to put himself
under a heavy debt, as for an education, or
for land, or for a home; but the debt-habit
is the twin brother of poverty.

(6.) Thrift must have a sufficient motive.
There is none a young man feels so keenly,
if once he will think so far, as the honorable place assigned to men of substance.
No man is quite respectable in this nine-
teenth century who has not a bank account.
True or false, high or low, this is the solid
fact, and, for one, I do not quarrel with it.
As most of us are situated in this world, we
must win this place and pay its price. The
common cry of "a good time while we are
young" is not the price nor the way. Mr.
Nasmyth, of England, an inventor and
holder of a large fortune made by himself,
says, "If I were to compress into one sentence the whole of my experience, and offer
it to young men as a rule and certain re-
·eipt for success in any station, it would be
comprised in these words, Duty first, pleasure second! From what I have seen of
young men and their after progress, I am
satisfied that what is called ' bad fortune,'
ill luck,' is, in nine cases out of ten, simply
the result of inverting the above maxim."

"Serve a noble disposition, though poor,' says George Herbert; "the time comes when he will repay thee."

We cannot properly leave our subject until we have referred to spending, for thrift consists in the putting out, as well as the ingathering, of money. It decides how, and to what extent, we shall both spend and save. We must leave ample room for the play of generosity and honor; we must meet the demands of church and home and community with a wise and liberal hand; we must preserve a keen and governing sense of stewardship, never forgetting the ultimate use of money, and the moral and intellectual realities that underlie life. This matter of thrifty saving is purely instrumental, simply to bring us into circumstances where self-respect, a sense of independence and of usefulness, are possible; or, putting it finer, we save to get into the freedom of our nature. Were the wisdom of the whole subject gathered into one phrase, it would be, When young, save; when old, spend. But each must have something of the spirit of the other; save generously, spend thriftily.

If I were to name a general principle to

cover the whole matter, I would say, *Spend upward*, that is, for the higher faculties. Spend for the mind rather than for the body; for culture rather than for amusement. The very secret and essence of thrift consists in getting things into higher values. As the clod turns into a flower, and the flower inspires a poet; as bread becomes vital force, and vital force feeds moral purpose and aspiration, so should all our saving and out-go have regard to the higher ranges and appetites of our nature. If you have a dollar, or a hundred, to spend, put it into something above the average of your nature that you may be attracted to it. Beyond what is necessary for your bodily wants and well-being, every dollar spent for the body is a derogation of manhood. Get the better thing, never the inferior. The night supper, the ball, the drink, the billiard table, the minstrels, — enough calls of this sort there are, and in no wise modest in their demands, but they issue from below you. Go buy a book instead, or journey abroad, or bestow a gift.

I have not urged thrift upon you for its own sake, nor merely that you may be kept

7

from poverty, nor even for the ease it brings, but because it lies near to all the virtues, and antagonizes all the vices. It is the conserving and protecting virtue. It makes soil and atmosphere for all healthy growths. It favors a full manhood. It works against the very faults it seems to invite, and becomes the reason and **inspiration of generosity.**

V.

SELF-RELIANCE AND COURAGE.

"And having done all, to stand. Stand, therefore."
ST. PAUL.

" 'Hell (a wise man has said) is paved with good inten-
tions.' Pluck up the stones, ye sluggards, and break the
devil's head with them."   *Guesses at Truth.*

"A mass, that is to say, collective mediocrity." — JOHN
STUART MILL.

"This above all: to thine ownself be true ;
And t must follow, as the night the day,
Thou canst not then be false to any man."
                                    Hamlet, i. 3.

V.

SELF-RELIANCE AND COURAGE.

So far we have spoken chiefly of conduct; in this chapter we speak of that interior thing that we call *selfhood* or *personality*. To get a clear, full sense of it is a great achievement, leading, as it does, to this quality or state of self-reliance. No man is self-reliant, or has intelligent courage, until he has come to a thorough sense of himself; not in any way of conceit or self-complacency, but by a deliberate survey and examination of himself, as if from the outside.

I think we may all agree with Humboldt that the aim of man should be to secure " the highest and most harmonious development of his powers to a complete and consistent whole; " or, as we said in the first chapter, "to make the most of himself." This is the specific work of civilization, to get the individual out of the mass and exalt him into personality. In savagery one is the duplicate of another. In civilization there is variety, or rather individuality, in the exact degree of the civilization. It comes about, as Mr. Mills tells us, through "freedom and variety of situations." Freedom takes off the restraints, so that whatever is in the man comes out. Civilization offers the variety of situations needful for confirming the individual traits. Thus there will be the most of strong, distinct character where there is the largest freedom and the most complex civilization. In simpler form, freedom gives us a chance; civilization stimulates us.

Other things, indeed, help to bring out individuality. Necessity spurs a man, and opportunities allure him. Both have had full play in this country. Poverty on one hand, and ungathered wealth on the other hand, — these have largely created the American type. Hence in a new country almost every man is what is called "a character." I think I noticed in California a sharper individuality than I observe in New England. The Englishman feels uncomfortably the broad and pronounced diversity of character he finds here, and **we** are obliged to confess that English society is just a little insipid from lack of it.

Religion also influences individuality. A superstition, a fixed form, a false faith, or a false rendering of the true faith, represses individuality. Idolaters and bigots resemble one another and are herd-like, but a faith like Christianity that is full of freedom, and is throughout keyed to deliverance, stimulates individuality. All along it has blossomed out into great original characters, — poets, statesmen, inventors, navigators, explorers, philanthropists. It was the secret of the Reformation that it restored to Christianity its normal order of freedom, long interrupted; when the pressure was taken off, all Europe burst into a brilliancy of thought and discovery such as the world had never seen. The literature of the Elizabethan age outranks that of Greece, not in perfection of form, but because it is instinct with a freedom and individuality not to be found in the ancients. Shakespeare may not be so great an artist as Æschylus, but he stimulates character as the Greek did not. I would like to remind young men in these days of insinuating, slighting infidelity, that the glory and force of modern civilization is the direct and logical outcome of Christianity. Its root-idea is *deliverance*. It first freed the human mind and then inspired it. It is something more than a matter of church and Bible; it is a life-giving spirit; it is an atmosphere; it is the soul of the world.

Race also has much to do with individuality. The blood that has force and courage in it produces the widest variety of character. It is significant that Christianity allies itself most readily to the strongest races, entering into them as quicksilver mingles with gold. The strong race opposes it at first with the stoutest will, and questions it with the profoundest interrogation, but still accepts it, because, at bottom, they sympathize. A weak race debases Christianity when it receives it, it cannot stand up under its stout duties; but the strong race takes it at its full measure.

This Anglo-Saxon blood of ours, with its refining strain of Norman, is the best in the world. It contains the virtues, and holds the vices as alien. It honors marriage and the home; it speaks the truth; it is honest; it is rich, comprehensive, charged with the widest possibilities. Its inmost quality is *force*, hence its clearest exponent is individuality. It tends to erect each man into a full-rounded person, whence comes liberty; for liberty is but the assertion of personality, with its rights and obligations. Such it has been of old and hitherto; let us hope that it will never lose this quality. Some one, I have forgotten who, has pointed out the significant fact that the god of our Scandinavian ancestors was not a Zeus hurling thunderbolts, but a Thor wielding a hammer; the Greek god shed arrows of fate; the Scandinavian beat down obstacles. An old Norseman, not mythologic, had for a crest a pick-axe, with the motto, " Either I will find a way or make one." And another said, "I believe neither in idols nor demons; I put my sole trust in my own strength of body and soul."

Just because the main quality of this blood is *force*, it retains this characteristic. Not every youth, with this forceful blood in his veins, carries Thor's hammer in his hand, but it is hidden somewhere about him. To get it into the strong right hand, where it can be wielded against the obstacles in the way of manhood, is the business before us.

When one rides through Italy and sees the brawny peasants stretched at ease by the roadside, one reflects that they have a justification in their blood. But a lazy, listless, forceless Anglo-Saxon is a contradiction to his own nature.

The most notable exhibitions of this blood, I think, are to be seen in its emigrations. A factory stretching across a valley indicates energy, but it does not reveal the particular quality of self-reliance as does the emigration of a man from the East to the frontier. The ancient emigrations were in masses ; the Anglo-Saxon does not wait for his neighbor, but takes counsel with himself, gathers together his family, and starts. Men do few braver things. I have never been prouder of my race than when I have come across, perched upon a swell of endless, desolate prairie in Nebraska, or hidden in some remote glen of the Sierras, the rough dwelling of a white-skinned settler, come there in the mighty strength of his self-reliance to build a home and hammer out a fortune with this same hammer of Thor. He is not a Mexican wandering with his herds, or "white trash" crowded to the frontier, but one of Bacon's "found

ers." All English history is behind him
and in him. He not only wins a living, but
subdues nature to his use and taste, and
makes soil and tree and ore tributary to his
grandly-conceived selfhood. He is a person — quite conscious of the fact; he wants
what belongs to a man, and, by the aid of
Thor's hammer, he will get it. Put a few
of these Anglo-Saxons down anywhere on
the continent, and forthwith they bring all
civilization to their doors.

Another feature of this civilization is its
expansive character, its tendency to com-
plexity, adding something new and perma-
nent every year. What it will attain to
when it has cleared all traditional obstacles
out of its way, and got into full freedom, is
beyond conception, because we have no conception of what is in man.

The thing I wish to get before young men
is, that they are summoned by inheritance
to a very lofty type of self-reliance and
manhood. But we sometimes fail of our
birthright. Other influences may work
against inborn tendency and force, and all
good things need culture. Necessity is the
spur to self-reliance; a noble pride and self-
respect are its atmosphere. Where there is

wealth the spur is apt to lose its sharpness and often self-respect is smothered under an accumulation of social influences.

My first direct word on the subject will be an appeal to young men to realize, each one for himself, that he is a *person.*

It is not every man who has said to him·self, " I am I ; I am not another, but I am myself." There are many who have not yet ascertained whether they are them-selves or some one else, and are quite as often one as the other ; many who do not get themselves detached from the mass of humanity, but live and act out of the com-mon stock of thought and feeling. When one agrees with everything I say, however carelessly I am talking, there is really but one of us. When Hamlet likened the cloud to a camel, a weasel, and a whale, and Polonius assented, there was but one person in the colloquy ; Polonius was no·body. To be a person, to have opinions and respect them, — this is something at once necessary and difficult, because at the same time a young man should heed and value the opinions of others, and steer wide of the slough of conceit. At the one ex-treme is the young man who agrees with

everybody, and goes with the crowd; at
the other extreme is one who knows everything and has settled all questions. The
latter may be the more odious at present,
but he will turn out better. His mates will
kick a part of his folly out of him, and contact with the world will wear away the
rest, leaving him a substantial person, while
the other, having no inherent shape, will be
moulded over and over to the end. He is
pious or wicked, Republican or Democrat,
liberal or bigot, according to the strongest
influence; the better reason has little weight
with him. Without doubt, one should hold
himself open to all good influences, but the
main question, after all, is whether one is a
mind to be convinced, or simply a mass to
be moulded and attracted. Every public
speaker knows that those who flutter about
him with readiest assent are not the ones
best worth convincing. I have little fear
for the self-opinionated young man. The
kind wise world has rods in keeping that
will take the conceit out of him. I fear for
him who goes with the crowd and draws his
opinions and sentiments from the common
stock. I hate to hear a young man say,
" They all do it," — a very shabby and

odious phrase. I hate to see a young man
jump into the current that happens to be
nearest, or just now most impetuous, —
whether it be good or bad, bicycle or Bernhardt, — and float with it for sake of the
company. It were better to be borne by
some stream of native feeling or personal
conviction, or to stand stock still while the
mindless crowd sweeps by. One should always question the prevailing *craze*, whatever it is, till he finds out if it has a reason
for *him* in it. I think if President Garfield's
time in college had been the bicycle era, he
would have been the first or the last to ride.
Either decision would have been from a personal reason. It is true that men move in
masses, that there is a gregarious instinct,
that great passions and purposes often make
whole populations as one man, but they are
movements that need to be carefully scrutinized. Those that have swept over our
country have not been very creditable, — a
dancer, a singer, an author who abused us,
a political adventurer, and just now an act-
ress whose son addresses her as " *Mademoi-
selle ma mère.*" Taglioni and Jenny Lind
and Dickens and Kossuth and Bernhardt
do not represent the highest forces in the

moral and intellectual world, but each has forced us to wear national sackcloth. I do not urge stolid insensibility to a prevailing enthusiasm. There is no objection to marching in a procession and throwing one's cap in air, but it is imperative that one should know why he does it. Still, marching in a procession is not the noblest way. One admires rather the self-poise of Fichte who kept at his books while the drums of Napoleon were sounding in his ears. Napoleon might be a very grand phenomenon, as he admitted, but he — Fichte — was also a phenomenon that he felt bound to respect. As a rule, resist the gregarious habit; suspect the crowd, and before you march in companies of whatever sort, find out if you are marching to please yourself or the captain. There is a great deal of organization and association of this sort, for the delectation of the leaders at the expense of subordinates. It is well to say of them, " I will consult *myself* on this matter; I will find out if it is agreeable and wise for this person that I am."

The heaviest charged words in our language are those two briefest ones, *Yes* and *No.* One stands for the surrender of the

will, the other for denial; one for gratifi-
cation, the other for character. Plutarch
says that " the inhabitants of Asia come to
be vassals to one only, for not having been
able to pronounce one syllable, which is
No." A stout *No* means a stout character;
the ready *Yes* means a weak one, gild it as
we may.

Practically, an attitude something like
this is wise: when a proposal is made,
consider it probable that there is as much
reason for refusing as for assenting. Will
you ride with me, drink with me, play with
me? For such questions and all others
have the No as convenient as the Yes. Indeed, when one thinks of the power of fashion and custom, it seems well to have
the No somewhat readier. The vices are
hardly more the result of appetite than of
custom. There have been periods and com-
munities in which nearly all were pure and
temperate; it was the custom. The thing
to be feared for young men at present is
the general understanding of what is cus-
tomary in the habits of certain circles of
their number. There is fearful power in
those four little words, " They all do it."
To resist the crowd, to hold the scales of

right and wrong in your own hand, to realize that whole masses may go wrong, —
that common custom may be vile, to stand
erect and within the inclosure of your self-
respect, this is a prime feature of manhood.

We must now look somewhat into the
methods of the culture of this brave quality

(1.) Education, of course, is its essential condition. The ignorant herd together,
think, feel, act alike ; but your trained man
suspects the crowd. He feels its encroach-
ments on his personality. He fears lest it
may steal his decision away from him by
brute force. He is sufficient to himself, and
stands on his self-grounded reasons and
habits. But while this process of education is going on that is to bring us into full
self-reliance, we must help it in special
ways.

(2.) Secure for yourself some regular
privacy of life. As George Herbert says,
" By all means, use sometimes to be alone."
God has put us each into a separate body.
We should follow the divine hint, and see
to it that we do not lapse again into the
general flood of being. Many persons cannot endure being alone; they are lost un-

8

less there is a clatter of tongues in their ears. It is not only weak, but it fosters weakness. The gregarious instinct is animal, — the sheep and deer living on in us; to be alone is spiritual. We can have no clear personal judgment of things till we are somewhat separate from them. Mr. Webster used to say of a difficult question, "Let me sleep on it." It was not merely for morning vigor, but to get the matter at a distance where he could measure its proportions and see its relations. So it is well at times to get away from our world — companions, actions, work — in order to measure it, and ascertain our relations to it. The moral use of the night is in the isolation it brings, shutting out the world from the senses that it may be realized in thought. It is very simple advice, but worth heeding. Get some moments each day to yourself; take now and then a solitary walk; get into the silence of thick woods, or some other isolation as deep, and suffer the mysterious sense of selfhood to steal upon you, as it surely will. Pythagoras insisted on an hour of solitude every day, to meet his own mind and learn what oracle it had to impart.

(3.) I name a very delicate point when I say, Cultivate a sense of personal dignity, — have bounds to familiarity. *Noli me tangere* — touch me not — is the utterance of a divine dignity. There is a subtle law by which greatness and excellence create a sense of separation. Refined manners forbid excessive familiarity, not simply as good manners, but because they contribute to selfhood. Hence the well-bred scrupulously respect each other's persons, down to the smallest particular. The very touch of the hand is instinct with delicate respect. No self-respecting man will suffer his body, or mind, or soul to be slapped on the back. Thus instinct and manners unconsciously guard personality, and secure to it room and air for growth.

(4.) Do not fear unpopularity. I do not say, court it, but, do not think much about it, nor dread it, if it comes through the assertion of your manhood. There is no time when the pressure of opinion is so strong as in early life. It is something fearful in its power in college, and where e else young persons are brought into close and daily contact. When a young man says of another, "He is popular," he says what he considers the best possible thing; but if " unpopular," the worst. I do not deny that there may be some reality of truth in this; but I protest against the slavishness it begets. To court popularity, to unduly dread the loss of it, is a denial of selfhood. It puts the standard of judging in another instead of retaining it in yourself. You like the good opinion of others; it is well; but first have a good opinion of yourself. It is well to respect others; very true; but first respect yourself. " If I do so and so, what will others think of me?" But what will you think of yourself? " I shall lose my place in society, if I refuse to do this or that." But is it worse than being turned out of yourself? " I fear I shall be unpopular." Fear rather being unpopular with yourself, for the soul of man is a sort of community; conscience, taste, self-respect, will, honor, judgment, — these are its citizens, whose suffrages are more to be desired than of the whole world beside.

To make popularity a guide is to come into middle life weak, and into age crippled. Self evaporates under the process, and when the flattering voices have died out, — there being no longer anything to appea

to them, — emptiness and weariness are all
that remain. There is no old age that is
so horrible as that of one who has lived on
popular applause. Even religion cannot
comfort one who has frittered away his
selfhood in a steady strife after popularity;
the very mechanism by which it operates is
gone.

(5.) Keep steadily before you the fact
that all true success depends at last upon
yourself, — trite to weariness, I acknowl-
edge, but one of those eternal truths to be
kept before us as we heed gravitation and
appetite. The tritest is always the truest.

By nature we are weak; our destiny is
to become strong; but we shun destiny, and
lean to our first characteristic. Who will
help me? What can I depend on? These
are our first natural questions. But we do
not get on the track of success until we drop
all such questioning, and begin to realize
that we must depend upon ourselves. By
success I mean a full manhood and its inherent peace. This is not possible until
one has planted himself upon his own powers and begun to work from them. He
may have money, friends, chances, good fortune, but that which underlies achievement

is the ability of the man himself. If success comes from without, it will be fictitious,
and will fail to make returns of happiness.
When it flowers out of one's energies, it is
a vital and ministering thing. Sir Fowell
Buxton — as substantial a citizen as England has produced in the generation —
said, "The longer I live, the more I am
certain that the great difference between
men, between the feeble and the powerful,
the great and the insignificant, is energy,
invincible determination. That quality will
do anything that can be done in this world;
and no talents, no circumstances, no opportunities, will make a two-legged creature a
man without it." In the same strain, President Porter: "Energy, invincible determination, with a right motive, are the levers
that move the world."

It is hardly necessary to say that self is
the only certain reliance. Money, family,
friends, circumstances, — these come and go
on the uncertain tide of time. The old
Norseman was right: on neither idols nor
demons, upon nothing but the strength of
his own body and soul, would he depend.
There must be, however, a self to depend
on. Self is not a whim; it is not im

pulse, nor ambition, nor flux of motives, but a substantial person, grounded in intelligence and will and moral sense.

I have not distinguished between self-reliance and courage, because they so interpenetrate each other. Courage may be regarded as the refinement of self-reliance, — the spirit-side to that of which self-reliance is the mind-side. When one says, Be self-reliant, he speaks to the will and judgment; when one says, Be courageous, he addresses the heart and spirit.

I would have you regard courage as nearly the supreme quality in character. One may get rich without it; one may live a "good easy" life without it, but one cannot live a full and noble life without it. It is the quality by which one rises in the line of each faculty; it is the wings that turn dull plodding into flight. It is courage especially that redeems life from the curse of commonness.

Before leaving the subject, I would like to set it distinctly against a disposition — growing somewhat common, I fear — to settle down into a purposeless enjoyment of the present: a life without earnestness or aspiration; a life that aims only at "having a good time," — a weak and beggarly phrase. The essential characteristic of this life is that it lacks courage, — the fine high spirit that disdains the common life, and dares the future for a nobler one; "the dauntless spirit of resolution," Shakespeare calls it. Is it true that young men are regarding life less ideally ? — that some mist, bred of prosperous times, has come into the air, obscuring the stars, and shutting the vision up to what is near and palpable ? Is Thor's hammer gone from our hands ? We will hope that it is but a mist that just now seems to be blinding the eyes of many, and that we shall again see young men drawn on by noble ambitions and high ideals.

It would be most incomplete to speak of courage and not refer to it in the hedged-in fields of life.

The burdens of life do not always fall upon the mature and aged. Life often takes on its most grievous and binding form in the young. Poverty, toil, sickness, imperfect education, premature responsibility, many of you, I know, bear these burdens. "What is all this to me ? I can attempt nothing great or high; I have no future but to keep

right on ; for me to aspire and plan is folly."
It may be so, but there is one thing you can
do, and it is the best thing any man can
do in this world, — you can keep up good
heart. This is courage, indeed : to look
into a dull future and smile ; to stay bound
and not chafe under the cords ; to endure
pain and keep the cheer of health ; to see
hopes die out and not sink into brutish de-
spair, — here is courage before which we
may pause with reverence and admiration.
It is so high that we link it with divine
things, carrying it quite beyond the sphere
of any earthly success.

VI.
HEALTH.

" Though the mills of God grind slowly,
   Yet they grind exceeding small;
  Though with patience He stands waiting,
   With exactness grinds he all."
                      LONGFELLOW.

" A sound heart is the life of the flesh."
                      SOLOMON.

" Though I look old, yet I am strong and lusty;
For in my youth I never did apply
Hot and rebellious liquors in my blood;
Nor did not with unbashful forehead woo
The means of weakness and debility;
Therefore my age is as a lusty winter,
Frosty but kindly."
                  As You Like It, ii. **1**

" Now, good digestion wait on appetite
And health on both ! "
                    Macbeth, iii. **4.**

VI.

HEALTH.

THE questions now coming into prom·inence pertain chiefly to social science. While there are political and religious questions that still vex and interest society, it is plainly to be seen that the eye of the world is fixed on this matter of living ; an *art* it is getting to be called. It has never yet seriously engaged the attention of the people. It is a new subject, and not yet fairly before us. The Greeks gave great heed to the individual body, and the Romans secured personal cleanliness by their vast system of baths, but neither seem to have had any conception of the public health; hence, with all their fine training and care of the body, their cities were subject to pestilence, and the average of life remained at a low point. The only successful attempt yet made to connect hygiene with the social order was made by Moses, who interwove its requirements with those of religion. If this critical generation could be diverted for a moment from the "mistakes of Moses" to some thought of his measures that were *not* mistakes, it would find itself in possession of some very suggestive facts. No nation has been so exempt from contagious and hereditary disease as the Jews, or can show vital statistics so favorable, or oftener blossoms out into a great original mind. There is no question but this racial vitality and toughness and exuberance is due to certain hygienic rules that Moses made effective and lasting by connecting them with religion, where, indeed, they belong. But, aside from the Jews (and in how many respects are they an exceptional people!), the art of health is a new subject. It is a singular fact that when men first reflectively examined themselves they began with their moral nature, then passed to their minds, and that is as far as they have got. Strange as it seems, it is the natural order, and shadows a tremendous truth, — morals first, mind next, body last. It is the eternal and fit order. Aristotle mapped out philosophy and morals in lines the world yet accepts in the main.

but he did not know the difference between the nerves and the tendons. Rome had a sound system of jurisprudence before it had a physician, using only priestcraft for healing. Cicero was the greatest lawyer the world has seen, but there was not a man in Rome who could have cured him of a colic. The Greek was an expert dialectician when he was using incantations for his diseases. As late as when the Puritans were enunciating their lofty principles, it was generally held that the king's touch would cure scrofula. Governor Winthrop, of colonial days, treated " small-pox and all fevers " by a powder made from " live toads baked in an earthen pot in the open air." And even now, in New England, where we split hairs in theology, and can show a philosopher for every square mile, at least one half of the treatment of disease is empirical ; that is, there is no ascertained relation between the remedy and the sickness ; it is largely a matter of advertisement and pretense. But a new day is dawning. Legislation is crowding the quack into the background, and the Board of Health is coming to the front.

The old Greeks put health so high as to

deify it.   Hygeia was a goddess, young and smiling and beautiful.   We are catching glimpses of her laughing face, and erelong we shall deify her.   It is a part of our sin that we are sick; it is a part of religious duty to be well.

I say all this to young men because it is well that they should be awake to the new phases of society that are coming on.   The special subjects to which intelligent men should have their eyes open are those pertaining to social science, the sanitary condition of towns and cities, all matters of drainage, ventilation, water-supply, house-building, as well as matters pertaining to personal health and vigor.   If any educated young man is looking about for a hobby, let me suggest that here is one that he can ride to better purpose than any other now to be laid hold of.

But the personal side of the subject is the one we have before us.   Evidently, nothing can be more personal, more literally and strictly vital, than bodily health.   It is the first and the perpetual condition of success. In any enterprise there are primary and secondary conditions affecting the result In making a voyage it is necessary first of

all to have a ship that will float and hold
together till the port is gained; it may
spread more or less canvas, be manned by
few or many sailors, be navigated with
more or less skill, be fast or slow, be driven
by wind or steam, — these are secondary
matters; the ship itself, staunch enough
to resist the waves, is the primary condition of the voyage. So in this enterprise
and voyage of life, a body sound enough
to hold together till the port of three-
score and ten is gained comes first, in
all wise and logical consideration. Talents, learning, aptitude, good chances,
energy, — these, according to the degree,
affect the voyage, and make it smooth or
rough, quick or slow, but they do not determine whether or not there shall be a
voyage. I do not say that these are to be
regarded lightly, or other than as great
helps, but I affirm that without bodily
health they are in vain so far as achievement is concerned. Energy, purpose, culture, enthusiasm, thrift, — these are the
engine that propel the man; but an engine
requires first of all proper bearings, a
frame stout enough to endure the strain of
its vibrations, and to convert its energy into

9

steady motion.   Professor Huxley goes too far, however, as he is very prone to do, when he says, " Give a man a good deep chest and a stomach of which he never knew the existence, and a boy must succeed in any practical career."   For it is a fact that a vast number of very worthless beings fulfill these conditions ; " animated patent digesters," Carlyle calls them, whose only achievements are the consumption of food and oxygen.   Brain and race and training have something to do with success in practical careers.   The captain on the bridge, the pilot at the wheel, and the engineer at the lever are conditions of the successful voyage, though the staunchness of the ship may be the primary condition.

It needs but a glance, however, at the men who have succeeded in any department to perceive that, as a rule, they have good bodies.   I do not say that all men who have achieved success have lived long, or been free from disease, but I assert that it is impossible to name a man great in any department of life who did not possess what a physician would call a *strong vitality*.   Many great men have died early and endured life-long disease, but a close physiological examination would show that they were largely endowed with nervous energy and usually with a good muscular system. I grant the rare exception, as a skiff may by good luck cross the Atlantic. Nature is not blind. She does not put great engines into weak ships. There is a fallacy in the common remark that the mind is too great for the body. A great mind may overwork and tear in pieces even a good body, but, for the most part, any body properly used and superintended is strong enough to uphold and do the work of the mind lodged in it. Man is one ; no line can be drawn between the working functions of body and mind. A part of all mental action is also physical action. Will is also a matter of nerves, energy is gradu- ated by the blood, and the finest thought stands with one foot upon tissue of brain. By its very definition high thought and large achievement imply a strong physical basis. Burns died at thirty-seven, and Byron at thirty-six, both of dissipation, but they had superb bodies, and, at first, exuberant health. Raphael and Robertson died at the same age with Burns, — one of malarial fever, and the other from over·

work and worry, — neither from physical necessity. Dr. Bushnell early induced consumption by excessive toil, but lived toiling on to seventy. When great men die early it is nearly always due either to abuse, or to something like an accident, for some diseases bear no relation to physical constitution. But great men do not die early. Dr. Dunglison says that the average longevity of the most eminent philosophers, naturalists, artists, jurists, physicians, musical composers, scholars, and authors, including poets who are not thought to be long-lived, is sixty-six years, — more than double the average length of human life. Such facts are usually regarded as showing that intellectual pursuits are favorable to longevity, but they rather show that great men have good bodies. A fine engine is favorable to the speed and safety of the voyage, but quite as much depends upon the build of the vessel, and even more upon how both are handled.

If now we look over the men who are considered successful in their departments, — professional, manufacturing, commercial, financial, — we shall find, with rarest exception, that they have certain physical char

acteristics which are the primary conditions
of a strong body and sound health. They
measure large around the chest; they have
depth of lung and good stomachs; their
muscular system is large and strong, or, if
small, it is fine in fibre and well knit together; they have a larger brain than the
average, and are without hereditary disease
that *early* impairs the chief functions. I do
not say that every man who has these characteristics achieves distinction, but that no
man achieves any considerable success who
is without them. There will always be
found a certain proportion of Carlyle's "animated patent digesters" with a perfect
physical make-up, but lacking in ways that
do not concern us here. Mr. Webster required to have his hats made for him on
account of the size of his head. The hatters
will tell you of many cases in which there
is no other likeness to the great senator.

You will also find that the measure of
success usually is determined by the manner
in which the owner of this well-endowed
body treats it. If the functional power of
lungs, or stomach, or nerves, is broken down
—often one and the same process — he
ceases in exact ratio to be an achiever. His

plans may go on themselves, but the fresh creative energy is graduated by his bodily condition. Force no longer goes into his schemes if it has passed out of his body.

Your physically weak man may get through life decently and honorably, but he never gets to be the head of anything, fore-man, or superintendent, or agent, or presi-dent; he never climbs, he never gets out of the crowd.

I do not expect any denial or doubt on these points, and have set them down only to get you to thinking on the subject. I fear, however, lest a nearly universal illusion may break its force. The first boast of childhood reaches a long way into manhood. However thin of limb and narrow of chest, the young man is always strong. The glory that men have ever put upon physical strength, and our instinctive sense of its excellence, so press upon us that we hate to confess our lack of it. Hence my readers may be saying, " This is not for me, but for the weakly ones," who are not anywhere to be found. Disenchantment is painful, but, in truth, every one is not a Hercules. The practical harm of this illusion is that we presume upon it, and infer that we can

endure any strain we may lay upon ourselves.

But what of athleticism ? Mr. Hughes,
its apostle, tells us in his last book that it
has come to be overpraised and overvalued.
It is undoubtedly a fine thing, but it has led
to an oversight of the wiser side of the matter, namely, the *preservation* and *care* of
the health, which is not entirely the same
thing as physical strength. It has also
reached a phase where the element of sport
and natural exhilaration is taken out of it.
They tell us that our national vice is *excess*,
— that we lack the sense of proportion.
Base-ball is no longer a minister of health
when a reporter sits by, and the cheers or
jeers of stake-holders follow the player
around the course. It is unfortunate that
this game, which Robert Collyer calls " the
healthiest and handsomest ever played," has
been pushed to such a feverish and wild
excess by stunning competition and accessories of gambling. A game loses its value to
health when its excitement is drawn from
any other source than from the game itself.
Stakes mean something more than healthful
exhilaration. Competitive walking and rowing are even more objectionable. They not

only engender positive disease, but the whole atmosphere, moral and social, is adverse to health. Hygeia does not welcome to her shrine the heroes of the bat and oar and ring. These sports may be used health-wise, but as soon as they involve the exertion called out by great public competition and the excitement of wager, they no longer minister to health. Unfortunately the temper of the age does not favor moderation. The element of play seems lost, and a hard vulgar pride of superiority to have taken its place. The self-sparkling water of natural play is not enough, but needs some devil's-powder of wager and newspaper report.

I think the votaries of athleticism run into another mistake by giving their interest to one thing; they can strike so heavy a blow, lift such a weight, walk so far; they are strongest in wrist, or leg, or loins. Those have been heard of whose superiority consists in the amount of liquor they can stand, under some delusion that it reflects credit on their brains, — plainly the idiotic side of the subject.

But special superiority does not constitute health. Nothing seems finer physically than the trained pugilist, but it is **well**

HEALTH. 137

understood that he dies early and commonly of consumption. Health is something different from strength; it is universal good condition; it is general vigor; it is that state of body in which every function works well.

Going a little farther in the way of criticism, too much value is attached to muscular strength, and too little to nervous energy. In some respects identical, they still represent distinct bodily forces. One is the power that *does*, the other *endures;* one strikes a single titanic blow, the other never tires; one wins a wager, the other wins a fortune and a name. Physical strength does not imply nervous energy, and though nervous energy implies a good body, it does not require great physical strength. Secretary Evarts is slender to frailness, but he has a nervous system that enables him to endure a harder and longer mental strain than any other lawyer at the bar of New York.

The gymnasiums at Yale and Amherst and Williams are quite necessary, and are justified by their results, but West Rock and Holyoke and Greylock are better. Climbing a ladder develops physical strength,

climbing a mountain feeds nervous energy.
Take two students: one can out-jump, out-
climb, out-lift his class; the other, having
slight ambitions of this sort, gets upon the
hills at every chance, "cutting" a recita-
tion now and then in the ardor of his long
rambles; at the end of twenty years it will
be found that the latter is the healthier
man.

In looking at men of marked attainment,
we find almost invariably certain physical
traits, but a closer look reveals this subtler
quality of nerve force or vitality. It is this
that makes the man what he is as a working power. Vitality is the measure of success. What vitality is we do not know.
We only know that its medium is the nervous system, and that it is fed and measured
by the assimilation of food and air. It has
a mysterious side, turned away from all
possibility of analysis, like the other side of
the moon. We only know that while it is
not nerve, nor oxygen, nor food, it is a force
that works through them. It may be a
spiritual thing, yet something that is graduated by its material relations. But, whatever it is, its degree or amount is determined
by the physical and nervous condition, as the

power of a telescope is determined by the size of its aperture. Nourish and strengthen your muscles and nerves and you increase your vitality, but it is the *vitality* that does the work, not the muscles or nerves. *The greatest amount of vitality,* — this is your requirement, young men! It is a trifling matter whether or not you can row, or bat, or walk to the admiration of a crowd and of yourself; but it is a matter of the greatest moment that you so use your body and regulate your life that you shall have your largest possible allowance of this mysterious thing called nerve-force, or vitality.

I am eager, however, to get the subject into a finer region of appeal. The possession of health should be a matter of straight, hearty, honest *pride.* I would have one hold himself ashamed who has not a man's share of manly vitality. If Providence denies it, it must be patiently endured. If one has inherited feebleness, let him blush for his ancestors. If one lacks it through personal fault, he must not only confess himself a guilty sinner, but guilty of a shameful sin. Bodily weakness minimizes a man; it is a subtraction, a derogation, a maiming in every part. It puts one below the average, makes one fractional, not a full counter in the game of life, small change to be disregarded in social estimates.

Despite the revival of athleticism and the spread of hygienic knowledge, the feeble young man is still to be seen, — not rarely; languid, listless, hesitating, forceless, thin-limbed, narrow-chested, uncertain, tremulous, the very thought of his conducting a business is a jest, though often he can drink, and smoke, and sit up of nights most admirably. I would like to reproduce on these pages Lockhart's picture of Wilson, — Christopher North, — simply to show what a superb thing a full vitality is : the grandest *physique* of any man of his century, robust, athletic, broad across the back, firm set upon his limbs ; in complexion a genuine Goth, with hair of true Sicambrian yellow falling about his shoulders in waving locks, his eyes of the lightest yet clearest blue, and blood flowing in his cheek with as firm a fervor as it did in his ancestral *Teutons*, who rushed to battle with laughter. De Quincey says that when Wilson was spending a vacation in the Highlands he would often run for hours over the hills, bare-headed, his long yellow hair streaming behind him, stretching out his hands and shouting aloud in simple exultation of life. There is a man for you — healthy, strong, vital!

To possess health in this fashion, to stand under the orderly heavens and amidst the harmonies of nature, light, air, earth, water, and growing things, all working in perfect unison, and feel that the harmony reaches to you; to feel that nature's laws are fulfilled in you as well as in tree, and planet, and ocean, — this is to share in the joy that underlies nature and is heard in her unvoiced hymn. Nor is it a smaller joy to stand before life with a consciousness of strength equal to its emergencies. The most exquisite feeling possible to man is the sense of ability to overcome obstacles; to face a wall and know that you can beat your way through it; to undertake an enterprise "of pith and moment" and know that you can carry it through to success; to come under an inevitable burden and know that you can stand erect. Facing life in this way is often regarded as a matter of mere spirit; but woe be to the man of spirit who undertakes great things without a well-flowered body; a dash, a flutter of unstrung nerves, ending in collapse, is all there is to relate.

Carlyle, in that wondrous wise talk of his to the students at Edinburgh, said: "Finally, I have one advice to give you, which is practically of very great importance. You are to consider throughout, much more than is done at present, and what would have been a very great thing for me if I had been able to consider, that health is a thing to be attended to continually; that you are to regard that as the very highest of all temporal things for you. There is no kind of achievement you could make in the world that is equal to perfect health. What to it are nuggets or millions?" Carlyle here voices the common feeling of overwhelming, irreparable mistake that vast numbers are called to undergo. Other mistakes may be overcome. Mind and moral nature are subject to the will, but a weakened body, who can correct that? There are for it no repentances and forgivings, but only the stern order of the material world, reaping after the sowing. No pangs of physical suffering would have wrung such words from Carlyle, but the fact that he had been crippled in his

work, that the clearness of his vision had
been dimmed, and that a hue not natural
to himself — a hue partial, distempered, mo-
rose — was spread over all that he had done.
It is late before we learn that the whole
of man goes into his work. Poet, or ora-
tor, or philosopher, or man of business, his
body follows him, and holds the pen, and
shapes the thought, and imparts its quality
to all that he does or says. An impaired
vitality of body implies an element of weakness in the undertaking to the end, and no
heroism of spirit, or strength of will, or in-
dustry can eliminate it.

If this discussion has had sufficient force
to excite an interest, it may lead to the
definite question, How shall we nourish
this vitality and health that Carlyle calls
"the highest of all temporal things"? I
hesitate to enter this field, since no writer
or speaker likes to antagonize his audience.
Besides, the way is somewhat worn, and you
have been driven or dragged over it so often,
and often in so repulsive ways, that I hesitate to class myself with your Mentors on
this subject. Still, trusting to a good understanding hitherto, I push on.

I think the best observers agree that

bodily vigor is a matter of preservation and steady care, rather than of special training. That is, God has given most of us health; the main thing is not to waste it. It is not something to be achieved, but something to be retained. If the practical wisdom of the matter were put into one phrase, I think it would be something like this: *Avoid whatever tends to lessen vitality.*

What are the things that do this?

(1.) It would be an unscientific treatment of the subject, if I did not lay heavy emphasis upon *tobacco*, as commonly used.

As in the chapter on *Thrift*, so here I speak of the use of tobacco in the single light of the subject in hand. There seem to me but three main objections to its use. It is an unthrifty habit; it is tyrannical, and so spreads out into the field of morals, where we will not follow it; and it is injurious to health. If these three points seem to you to cover nearly the whole sphere, I shall not deny it. Thrift, morals, health, — they are indeed somewhat broad!

Persons of certain temperament, and of rough out-of-door employment, may be exceptions to the extent that the injury is not perceptible. But taking life as we have it

—. with less and less of the phlegmatic temperament, and more and more of city life and indoor occupation, — the tobacco habit must be set down as injurious. It might not be so to any great degree if its use did not call into play that subtle law of increase that renders moderation a difficult thing to secure. Logically, there can hardly be any moderation in a habit so related to the will, for the habit itself is one of *indulgence*, a field from which the will is shut out; hence the only limit, ordinarily, is that imposed by satiety; the smoker stops when he does not care to smoke longer.

But there are physiological reasons why tobacco and alcohol create an increasing appetite. They are nerve-stimulants; stimulated nerves mean at last irritated nerves, and irritated nerves clamor forever. And being unnaturally irritated and stung into undue action they lose their force, which is a loss of vitality. This is what any physician will tell you, namely, that tobacco is a debilitant; that it weakens the nerve centres; that it lessens vitality; that it subtracts from energy; that, being weakened, it renders one more liable to disease; that it engenders certain ailments, and tends to

10

induce a certain condition the most remote
from that any man could wish.

(2.) The drinking habit is to be set down
as a great waster of vitality. The moderate
use of alcohol is a cheat. It is opposed
in its very nature to moderation. Morally and physiologically it is keyed to the
opposite of moderation. The exceptions are
the decoys without which the evil would
bag no game.

But the physiologists are practically
agreed that even a moderate use of alcohol
is injurious to vitality. Dr. Richardson, of
London, says, " It is the duty of my profession to show, as it can show to the most perfect demonstration, that alcohol is no necessity of man ; that it is out of place when
used for any other than a medical, chemical,
or artistic purpose ; that it is no food ; that
it is the most insidious destroyer of health,
happiness, and life." He says again :
" Among the chief sources of the reduction
of vitality to the low figure at which it
stands, alcohol stands first ; it kills in the
present, it impairs the vital powers in the
succeeding generations." " If England were
redeemed from its use," he says, " the vitality of the nation would rise one third in its

value." But the drinking habit in this dry, nerve-exciting climate of ours is far more injurious than it is in England. If it there reduces vitality a third in value, what must it do here? The simple fact for a rational being to consider and govern himself by is that every time he drinks a glass of liquor, whatever its per cent. of alcohol, *he lessens his vitality;* he has just so much less power to work with, less ability to endure, less nervous force for fine efforts, less toughness to put against difficulties, less time to live. What! if it be only beer? Yes! the verdict of science is absolute and final.

Does any one sing the praises of wine? Every generous heart has a chord that vibrates to that note; but, after all, the wine of *life* is better and more musical. Does any one speak of usage? I protest by all the glories of humanity against a fashion that overrides the welfare of humanity.

(3.) I come to points less emphatic, less familiar, also, as yet, but soon to engage practical attention. It is not a hundred years since Priestley discovered oxygen, and so run upon the fact that air robbed of it by breathing contains dangerous properties, a truth that has not yet reached general recognition. Sextons and mill-builders, and the entire in-door world, practically hold that one can live equally well anywhere outside of a vacuum. Oxygen is life, the gas it liberates is death. When you breathe air deficient in one and over-laden with the other you reduce vitality, and pave the way for disease. The melancholy feature of mill life — now coming almost into supremacy in numbers — is not low wages, but scant oxygen. An English physician says that " health is a thing absolutely unknown amongst English factory operatives."

In this respect many of you are shut out of any choice. I can only say, value every breath of pure air you can get, work in it if possible, sleep in it without fail, hesitate to stay where it is not, and, whenever it is possible, drink it in as it blows over summits of hills, and through moist woods.

(4.) Lack of sleep is a great waster of vitality.

Carlyle quotes the French financier with a sigh : " Why is there no sleep to be sold ? Sleep was not in the market at any price." Its lack is the tragical feature of broken health. " Chief nourisher in life's feast," the omniscient poet calls it. Never, except for the most imperative reason, should one break in upon that sacred process for which the sun withdraws itself and silence broods over the hemisphere. Its hours cannot be safely changed. Two young men, equally strong, work side by side; one sleeps early and long, the other retires late and irregularly. Apparently they get on equally well, but the physician will tell you that one is drawing on his stock of vitality, while the other keeps it full; in time one is bankrupt in health, the other rich.

Sleep is to be regarded as a divine thing; it is akin to creation. One should never pass into it without adoration; it is a return into the hands of God to be new-made, the tire and age of the day to be taken out, and freshness and youth wrought in.

> "Come, blessed barrier between day and day;
> Dear mother of fresh thoughts and joyous health!"

Or, more tenderly, with Allingham: —

> "Sleep is like death, and after sleep
>   The world seems new begun;
> While thoughts stand luminous and firm,
>   Like statues in the sun;
> Refreshed from supersensuous founts,
> The soul to clearer vision mounts."

The physiologist cannot explain it; all he knows is that, in some way, it renews vitality. To tamper with it, to defraud it, to take it fitfully, is to throw away life itself. It is a mistake to devote the hours up to midnight to work, or pleasure, or books. It may be a very innocent thing to dance at the right time and place, and in the right way and company, but to dance all night is to defraud life itself. Compare, in any matter requiring nerve and head, one who has slept all night with one who has spent a sleepless night and you will get an illuminating verdict on the value of sleep.

Business men who have borne the heavy cares of the last twelve years will assent when I say that the whole life, hygienically, should be ordered with regard to sleep. If one can sleep he can endure anything, he is every day a new man. Food, exercise, pleasures, hours, everything should be subordinated to securing sleep. No revival of troubles, no vexing questions should precede it. It should be as regular as the stars, and like the night itself in its solemn peacefulness.

(5.) I will only name sound digestion as fundamental to vitality, it being so well understood. The deadly effects of frying-pan and pie are no longer secrets. The hygienists are steadily telling us in the newspapers that we eat too much and too fast, that the national cooking is bad, that narcotics and stimulants and bad air and indolence and hurry and anxiety are foes of digestion. Professor Huxley encounters no denial when he makes a good stomach a condition of success in any practical career.

(6.) Nor will you expect me to do more than name those requirements of self-respect, as well as of health, the frequent bath, and that scrupulous care of the body that reaches up to religion.

As a piece of sanitary statistics, bearing on this and kindred points, I think the civilized world can offer nothing so remarkable as the following. I insert it for its suggestiveness, and also because it has not before been published. Seventy-five Chinamen in the employ of C. T. Sampson & Co., of North Adams, lost in four months but eight days, and no one man lost a whole day, showing an entire exemption from severe sickness; more than seventy-eight hundred consecutive working days and not an entire day lost by an individual. When taken in connection with the fact that these men daily took a sponge-bath, drank no alcohol, slept early and long, and ate good food, the figures turn into arguments and appeals.

(7.) There are hindrances to a strong vitality that are inseparable from life as it comes to most of us. Our working classes labor harder and longer than any other in the world, our business men have longer hours, our professional men give themselves less rest. There is a danger from over-work not to be forgotten; it is already being felt in a rapid increase of nervous diseases with their irresistible tendency to the use of narcotics and stimulants, and a ready susceptibility to malarial influences. Our climate does not admit of so hard labor as that of England, but the English operative works but five and a half days to our six, and the professional and business man begins late and stops early, making a sort of Sabbath of his evening.

(8.) Nothing more surely cuts away and undermines the vital forces than worry and anxiety, however caused. Happily, trouble is not native nor lasting in youth—touching it but lightly:—

> ' As night to him that sitting on a hill
> Sees the midsummer, midnight, Norway sun
> Set into sunrise.''

But as we descend from these glorious heights we encounter the inevitable cares and anxieties that are involved in the increased relations of life. It is a large part of what Sir Thomas Browne calls " the militia of life " to see to it that these cares do not break up the order either of soul or body. The practical lesson here is both religious and prudential. It says, live carefully, avoid needless entanglements, don't compromise yourself, keep a good conscience, have nothing in your life that requires concealment. Burdens and cares a man must have, but a true and simple habit of life, held to loftily and devoutly, will keep them from harming body or soul.

(9.) My last suggestion will, perhaps, have more novelty than any other before named. The passions of anger, hatred, grief, and fear are usually considered as belonging to morals, but Dr. Richardson puts them amongst the influences most destructive of vitality. " The strongest," he says, " cannot afford to indulge in them." Shakespeare, whom nothing escapes, speaks of envy as " lean-faced."

> " Heat not a furnace for your foes so hot
> That it do singe yourself."

When these great passions burn, the oil of life is rapidly spent. Hence, divine wisdom forbids hatred and anger, and divine love heals our griefs and fears, as hurtful alike to body and soul.

I cannot better end these suggestions than by quoting some words of Bacon, whose wisdom seems to comprehend every subject he touches. As if speaking to young men, he says, " It is a safer conclusion to say, ' This agreeth not well with me, therefore I will not continue it,' than this : ' I find no offense (or hurt) of this, therefore I may use it; ' that is, don't wait till you are hurt by a habit before giving it up, but find out its ordinary tendency, and act accordingly."

VII.

READING.

'Bring with thee the books." — St. Paul.

"These young obscure years ought to be increasingly employed in gaining a knowledge of things worth knowing; especially of heroic human souls worth knowing." — Carlyle.

" 'T would be endless to tell you the things that he knew
All separate facts, undeniably true,
But with him or each other they'd nothing to do;
No power of combining, arranging, discerning,
Digested the masses he learned into learning."

A Fab' for Critics.

"No man can read with profit that which he cannot learn to read with pleasure." — President Porter.

VII.

READING.

THE universal distribution of books has given rise to a new and distinct ambition that may be described as a desire for intellectuality. To be intellectual, or to be regarded as such, is certainly among the ambitions of modern society. The logic of it is plain: men do not like to be out of relations to great facts. The prominent figure, the strong party, the new discovery, fixes their attention and enlists their sympathies. Napoleon, simply by his outstanding greatness as a phenomenon, commands a homage from which our judgment dissents. The dignity and sense of reality that Milton throws about Satan has secured for him what may even be called respect.

Books are the great fact of modern civilization, its finest expression and summation. If we were to send to the next planetary neighbor our most representative thing I think it would be a book — Shakespeare, or the New Encyclopædia. But books stand for intellect; their source, their method, their reception is in the intellect. Thus, the whole atmosphere about them being intellectual they have come to stand for the thing itself, and to imply its possession on the part of all concerned with them.· It seems an incongruity when an ignorant person sells us a book. No one can afford to ignore this great latter-day fact. You will need to drop somewhat below the average of our American culture before you will find one who does not claim something of the spirit that surrounds books; very ill-founded, it may be, but very devoutly entertained. There is almost no conception of intellectuality apart from them; to know them is to be intellectual.

There may be some crudeness and misapprehension in this, but, on the whole, it is praiseworthy. It marks the full transition from animal to man. It points the way to better things, for when the masses actually think, all else of which the moralist dreams and the saint prays, will follow. Thought is the crucible in which all things are resolved and separated to their true issues.

What shall I read? Such is the question everywhere put by this new ambition. The question does not seem to me a difficult one, like that of amusements, but, on the contrary, too easy to admit of much discussion. It is like standing in an orchard laden with fruit; it is not a matter of choice, but of falling-to, and taking the best. The worm-eaten, the wind-blasted, the rotten, will of course be passed by.

I am not sure that any rule is of very great use except one, and that shall be negative: namely, read no books but the best. But this negative rule covers a vast field. The bad or indifferent books are more than the good; and reading, of course, bears the same proportion. A book once represented the inspiration and thought of its author; to-day it represents a price paid. The change and perversion is immense. The standard and spirit of literature are not drawn from genius and intelligence, but from the tastes and conceptions of the masses, — an inversion that demands unending protest. When the author abdicates in favor of the reader there is an end of literature. Even in children's books there is no need of descent. A child requires only plainness, never a dropping down. The great masterpieces in this literature — "Robinson Crusoe," Hans Andersen's Stories and those of our own Andersen, Mr. Scudder, — "Paul and Virginia," "Picciola," — "Arabian Nights " — appeal equally to young and old ; one never suspects in them that the author has left his highest plane. To make this distinction between the legitimate and the false is difficult until one's taste and judgment are established. But there are certain rules that come nigh to the matter.

(1.) Resolutely avoid the immoral literature that flood the news-stalls. One who reads in this direction reads himself into moral chaos and darkness; it is an unknowing, uneducating process. There is something peculiarly destructive in that knowledge of evil which comes through a book or picture. The direct sight and sound of it do not so wound and blast as does that apprehension of it gained by reading. It thus seems to get *into* the mind ; it entrenches itself in the imagination, where it stays and multiplies itself, breeding through the fancy, turning these noblest faculties in to ministers of perdition.

"Where such fairies once have danced
No grass will ever grow."

(2.) There is a class of periodicals,
weekly and monthly, of a higher grade,
printed in heavy type and with coarse,
startling illustrations, and filled with stories.
It is hard to determine whether the paper,
the type, the illustrations, or the matter, is
the shabbiest; all wear the broadest badge
of vulgarity. Not the worst feature is
their cheapness. They are not often immoral, but they lack absolutely and utterly
every positive element of true literature.
Their effect might be described as mental
obliteration. For reading may be an uneducating process, and lead to a reversal
of this intellectuality of which we spoke.
When the mind is steadily addressed in a
low and untrue way, when it is constantly
excited by false emotions and set to acting
in unreasonable ways, it loses its power to
guide and serve; *flabby*, perhaps, is the best
word to describe it.

I say, not only do not read this rubbish,
but read nothing in preference. The mind
will be stronger if left to itself and the
unlettered literature of sky, and field, and
forest, or even street, where, at least, you

11

will see true men and women, and real
transactions.   Rather than spend your Sun-
days with these sheets, go into the hills,
and hear what the winds and birds have to
say.

(3.) There is a class of books known as
the novels of the day; novels of adventure,
of society, and of high-wrought passion.
As a rule they are to be avoided on the
same ground that you decline to buy a fair-
looking garment when you have reason to
believe that its wool is shoddy and its silk
is cotton.   It is true that a great novel may
contain exciting adventure; in itself there
is no harm in thrilling events, for all fact
runs off into surprise.   A great novel may
depict society, and it is always animated by
a great passion, but it will be *true* in each
of these respects.   Such books are rare;
you may count their authors on your two
hands.   Nothing can make a book worth
reading in which the delineation of motives
and conduct is false to reality and nature.
If the adventure is excessive, if the delineation of society consists of human frailty and
in set in any other light than of condemnation, if that is set forth as common which is
exceptional, if the sentiment is morbid, if

the frailties of genius are made to override
the homely, every-day virtues, if exceptions
are made in favor of immorality, if the
whims of the author are set down as laws
of conduct, — let all such books go unread.
Among many good reasons, the main one is
that these characteristics have a common
root of untruth, while the first and absolute
requisite of a book is that it shall be *true.*
Nothing but truth can feed the mind — as
nothing else can please it, if it is a healthy
mind. It is truth that makes the essential
greatness of a book, — holding the mirror
up to nature, getting the reality of things
before the reader. Great masses of books,
nearly all the novels of the day, yield before this fundamental criticism. They have
one or both of two characteristics; the plot
turns upon a restlessness under, or violation of, marriage, or the tone is pessimistic,
namely, holding evil to be the law of society.
Occasionally a sweet, healthy novel slips
from the press, like one of Mrs. Stowe's, or
Mrs. Craik's, or MacDonald's, or Mrs. Whitney's, — but the great mass are such as I
have described. These books do not hold
the mirror up to nature, or to society, or to
the real currents of human thought; they

mirror the distorted notions of very con-
ceited persons of very shabby principles,
who find it easier to write down their own
vaporings than to study nature and society.

It is not pleasant to know that a vast
number of persons read little else but such
books as these. The frequent domestic tragedy, the discontent, the sentimentality, and
general hystericalness of thought and manners, are largely due to this overwrought and
shallow literature. It not only weakens the
fibre of the mind, but it induces a low standard of taste in everything else — amusements, religion, society.

But, you ask, how shall we know the
good books from the bad ? Just as you dis-
tinguish between persons, by reputation and
acquaintance. You are cautious in regard
to your company ; you make no acquaintance except on the strength of a proper introduction or general reputation. Use the
same rule with books. There is no necessity of reading the last new novel. If you
have any secret vanity in literary things, to
which I do not object, let me say (in a
whisper) that the proper thing is *not* to
read the last new book ; if you are tempted

to do so avoid mention of it, unless you would be thought a *parvenu* in these high realms. If your friend who "reads all the new books" is patronizingly surprised that you have not seen Zola, or Ouida's last, inquire how long since he has read "Henry Esmond," and the blush will be on the other cheek. An author very soon gets a reputation; go by it and make no adventures amongst the unknown. One should find his way in the literary world as he learns geography, by maps, and not by first-hand explorations. Emerson says, Wait a year before reading a new book; and Lowell : —

"Reading new books is like eating new bread,
One can bear it at first, but by gradual steps he
Is brought to death's door of a mental dyspepsy."

Occasionally an author enters at once into an assured and commanding place, as Ebers, who a year ago was nearly unknown in fiction, but is to be read with confidence.

What of newspapers and magazines? Read the former as a matter of business and necessity, and expect no advantage from them except as they report to you current events. I must know what is going on in the world, I buy the newspaper to tell me, and for no other reason. If the keen-eyed editor puts a few of the events together, and says they point in this or that direction, I thank him, but keep a look-out for myself. I ask of him chiefly facts, events, the daily history of the globe. As a mental discipline, the reading of newspapers is hurtful. What can be worse for the mind than to think of forty things in ten minutes? It is commonly understood that the great editors pursue a definite course of continuous study for the sake of mental integrity, and as a defense against the dissipation of their daily work.

Magazines, the monthlies and quarterlies, fall into a different category. They often contain solid and thorough pieces of thought and information, and are the channels of much of the best current literature. But beware of the magazine story, except it be from a master; and as for serials — to read a good story thus is a self-inflicted cruelty.

And what of the novel? Almost the only limits left about novel-reading are those of likes and dislikes, rules and standards everywhere else, but none here. Highly moral people read very immoral books ; re-

fined people read vulgar ones ; fastidious
people welcome to their minds characters
whom they would turn out of their parlors.
Children go to school for study and come
home to serials, a veritable Penelope's-web
process. The whole matter is at very loose
ends, and needs to be brought under some
law of reason and consistency.

As a first step in this direction, read but
few novels, and with carefulest selection,
and at decided intervals of time.

I would have two objects in view, va-
rying them according to the end, namely,
amusement, and knowledge of life.

Every hard worker is entitled to a holiday now and then. Treat yourself to a
novel as you take a pleasure trip, and, because you do it rarely, let it be a good one.
We have a friend who prays that his life
may be spared till he has read all of the
Waverley; for he will not dull his interest
in one by soon taking up another. Having
selected your novel with something of the
care you would choose a wife, give yourself
up to it ; lend to its fancy the wings of your
own imagination ; revel in it without re-
straint ; drink its wine ; keep step with its
passion ; float on its tide, whether it glides

serenely to happy ends, or sweeps dark and tumultuous to tragic destinies.

Such reading is not only a fine recreation, but of highest value, especially to business men. It cultivates what the American lacks by nature, and doubly lacks through social atmosphere, namely, *sentiment;* by which I mean responsiveness to the higher and finer truths.

But the main use of the novel is to unfold character and society; this is its vocation, — to depict life. It may be historical, domestic, social, psychological, political, or religious, but its theme is *life.* Its value consists in the fidelity of the picture and the literary charm with which it is invested. When I read a novel of Thackeray my knowledge of man is increased. I get broader views of humanity. I see what a wide, deep, complex thing life is. Hence I will read no novels but the best, since they alone can show me life as it is; and above all things I must not think of life falsely. We might live virtuously while holding that the world is flat, but not if we were deceived as to the shape and proportions of man. Ptolemaic astronomy were better than unnatural fiction.

If you ask who these best novelists are, I will venture to name those who, at least, head the column. Pardon the dry list: Scott, Cooper, Thackeray, Mrs. Stowe, Dickens, "George Eliot," Hawthorne, MacDonald, Miss Brontë, Miss Edgeworth, Mrs. Whitney, Jane Austen, Bulwer, Lever, Mrs. Gaskell, Trollope, Charles Kingsley, Black, Howells, Blackmore; of foreign authors, Victor Hugo, Auerbach, Ruffini, and Ebers.

Surely, here are enough for the longest life. There is a vast number of good novels besides these, — correct in presentation, sound in sentiment, instructive, entertaining. I do not say, Don't read them; but consider the matter well. I once asked our widest and most thorough reader of English literature if he had read a certain popular novel. He replied, "I only read the saints." I wondered why I had read it, when I, too, might have read the saints.

But the novel is the holiday of literature; let us come down to its every-day features. Here the first question will be, What shall determine my reading?

(1.) While you are to read nothing that does not interest you, something besides interest must decide what the book shall be. If the interest always coincided with what is best, it were well indeed; but pleasure rarely coincides wholly with judgment. Therefore, I say, read what is best for you, what will teach you something; read to know, to think; but you must also be interested. It is not necessary to descend in the character of one's reading to find zest; it may be found by turning aside. Descents, everywhere and in all things, are to be avoided. You may take no interest in Hume's "History of England;" try Froude's, or Knight's with its rich illustrations, or Dickens's "Child's History"— a book for all. Another method would be to read those novels of Scott that touch upon the various reigns and the historical plays of Shakespeare, — the best of all English histories, truest to the time and freest from bias. Starting with one of these, or "The Abbot," or Kingsley's "Hereward," pass to the more accurate, but no truer form in the pages of Macaulay and Freeman and Green. Ancient history is proverbially dull; but we are now getting it in charming and trustworthy form from Ebers. Still, we must not forget Plutarch, — "the prattler

in history," Emerson calls him, — the seren-
est and most stable figure in the whole
world of books.

So of biography. The Lives of Dr. Arnold and Sir Fowell Buxton may be dull
to you, but Smiles's " Life of Stephenson,"
or Hughes's " Alfred the Great," or Irving's
" Columbus," cannot fail to stir your interest.

Your religious friend puts into your hand
a volume of sermons, — very good, doubtless,
but to you "dry as summer dust." Ask
him for those of Phillips Brooks or Robertson, and in time you may come to
like those of Bushnell and Liddon, and
even Mozley. Perhaps you are skeptical,
and he gives you a volume of Evidences
— Paley or McCosh; but it is too exact-
ing in its thought, and fails to hit your
mood or temper of mind. Try, instead,
" Ecce Homo," or Brooks's " Influence of
Jesus," or the " Life of Robertson," or
Hughes's " Manliness of Christ," — books
instinct with fresh and noble feeling.

Still, an earnest reader must have a
deeper motive than interest. One must
not pet one's self in this matter. It is a
serious part of life's business, and must

be conducted upon sound principles and with resolute firmness.

(2.) Read for general culture. As one studies grammar for correct speech, or travels to learn the ways of the world, or mingles in society for polish, so one ought to read for a certain dress and decoration of the mind. It is not creditable — it is like excessive rusticity in manners and attire — to lack a certain knowledge of English literature. It is unkind and embarrassing to others not to be able to respond, with some degree of intelligence, to what they assume to be well known by all. I hardly know how you manage it when the young lady fresh from Vassar or Wellesley asks you which of Shakespeare's plays you most admire. I can assure you that no disquisition upon Buffalo Bill will blind her to the fact that you are unfamiliar with Hamlet. To this end of simple fitness for society, one should read parts, at least, of certain authors. It will not be amiss to indicate the lowest requirements, especially as they are available by all: a part of Shakespeare's plays, — "Hamlet," "Macbeth," "The Tempest," "The Merchant of Venice," and "Julius Cæsar;" Milton's shorter poems and the first two books of "Paradise Lost;" 'Pilgrim's Progress;" Dr. Johnson's "Lives of the Poets;" the poems of Goldsmith, Lamb's essays; Burns; Wordsworth's ballads, sonnets, and "Ode on Immortality;" parts of Byron's "Childe Harold;" a few of the shorter poems of Coleridge, Shelley, Keats, and Cowper; four or five of Scott's novels; some of the essays of Macaulay and De Quincey; Tennyson, Mrs. Browning, and Ruskin in part; some history of England, — Knight's or Green's; the one or two best works of the greater novelists; some definite knowledge of our own authors, — Irving, Cooper, Hawthorne, Prescott, Motley, Bancroft, Mrs. Stowe, Emerson in "English Traits," and our five great poets. So much we need to read before our minds are well enough attired for good society; otherwise we must appear in intellectual corduroy and cow-skin.

(3.) Read somewhat in the way of discipline. This may take you in a direction contrary to your tastes. You are doubtless fond of the novel, but it is not enough to say, I will read only such as are good. You require another kind of book, — an essay, a treatise, a review article, a history or biography, — something that may not *win* attention, which, therefore, you must *give*. The chief, if not only value, of mathematics as a discipline lies in its cultivation of the habit of *attention;* close consecutive thought held to its work by the will. I do not see why the same end may not be reached by reading, if it is done in this way of attending, — stretching the mind over the subject so as wholly to cover and embrace it. When one reads out of mere interest, and without exercise of the will, the mind gets flabby. There can be no strength where there is no will. The omnivorous reader is often weak and essentially ignorant. There is such a thing as being the slave of books; true reading implies mastery.

(4.) Read variously. The secret of true living is to have many interests. Think with the astronomer and with him whose talk is of manures and soils; with your neighbor and with him at the antipodes; with lawyer and doctor and minister; with merchant and manufacturer; with high and low. It is a rich and various world we are in ; we should touch it at as many points as possible. The literature that mirrors it is also rich and various; wider even than the world, since it contains the past, and also the possible. Man is coördinated to this richness and variety; so far as may be, he should draw upon the whole of it, for he needs it all to fill his own mould. I distrust the man of one book, even if it is the best of books, or of one class of books. A lawyer may get no direct aid from Tennyson in pleading cases but you may more safely trust your case with him — if it be a large one — because the fact of reading such an author indicates that he covers more space in the world of thought. A physician cannot study human nature in Shakespeare without getting a conception of man helpful in his practice. He fails oftenest in an imaginative grasp of his business; Shakespeare is the best teacher of breadth. All other things being equal, trust the lawyer who reads books of imagination, the physician who studies books unfolding human nature, and the preacher who does not confine himself to theology.

In the recent works of English scholars, whether on natural science, medicine, history, political economy, biography, or theology, you will observe that without exception they are wide readers outside of their departments. It not only imparts a charm and richness to their style, but makes their books more trustworthy, since it shows that they think in various directions, and therefore are better entitled to their opinions.

There is special need of wide reading at present, because of a certain antagonism between the great departments of thought. Physics and ethics, science and theology, stand opposed. But the reader, whose business it is to "circumnavigate human nature," cannot recognize such antagonism; Trojan and Tyrian must be regarded alike. It is not scholarly to read science, and not morals: Tyndall, and not Dr. Hopkins; Spencer, and not President Porter; Darwin, and not Martineau.

You will find, after a time, that one of the chief delights in reading consists in substantiating what you find in one department by what you find in another. The secret of the charm lies in the fact that one is following the hidden threads that bind the creation into unity. Material things are the shadows of spiritual things; the law of the planet is in the flower and in man. The intelligent reader has no keener enjoyment than in the surprise felt as he comes on these analogies. As an illustration, — in our last chapter, the passion of anger was spoken of as hostile to physical vitality. We learned that these wires that we call *nerves* are never so strong after they have once trembled with rage, — a fact taught by physiology. But in the Book of morals we are forbidden to hate, and anger is declared to be folly. As we come across it in physics, we say, How wise! When we find it in ethics, we say, How gracious! It is a law that allies itself throughout each sphere with highest good. But what shall we say when we place the two revelations side by side, — the body uttering its physical law and the spirit its moral law in utter accord, — heaven and earth agreeing to one issue! The charm of such interwoven truth is the reward of the wide and impartial reader. But if you have a fancy or partiality, you may best feed it not by direct, but by general reading, for you will find it running as a thread through all literature.

(5.) Never read below your tastes. If a book seems to you in any way poor, coarse, low, or untrue, it may be passed by. There may be reasons why we should associate with low persons; we may influence them, but we cannot alter a book. The

12

first quality to be demanded of a book is
that it shall be *true ;* the second is that it
shall be *noble.* If there is laughter in it,
it must be the laughter of the gods. Books
of humor, especially those of American
origin, are to be carefully scrutinized, and
at most but "tasted." Those of Lowell
and Holmes are almost the only exceptions.

(6.) Read on a level with your author,
with no subservience, in a kindly critical
mood, — the author a person, yourself also
consciously a person.

I occasionally turn over the leaves of a
copy of "Tucker's Light of Nature," — as
solid and abstruse a book as one often encounters, — that was owned and annotated
on its broad margins by Leigh Hunt. It
is admirable to see how the airy poet kept
abreast of his robust author, challenging
his thought, denying here and agreeing
there. I have by me a copy of the "Life
and Letters of Henry More" annotated by
President Stiles; but the old New England
divine does not seem to have been abashed
before the great Platonist. Do not sit at
the feet of your author, but by his side;
trust him, but watch him. He has his
limitations and prejudices, and at some point

they may be narrower than your own. This is eminently necessary in reading such authors as " George Eliot," Emerson, Carlyle, and Matthew Arnold. The critical faculty is assisted by wide reading. We not only use our own judgment, but we learn to pit authors against each other: Emerson the transcendentalist against " George Eliot " the positivist; the spiritual Pascal against the materalistic Spencer. It is not necessary to agree wholly with any author; there is in each a limitation, a weakness, which is to be taken for granted. It is Shakespeare only who seems never to falter, never to go beyond or fall short.

(7.) Read in the line of your pursuit. If you build sewers or bridges, study up the Roman aqueducts. If you handle dyes, do not be ignorant of the Tyrian purple. The obvious effect of reading upon one's pursuit is that one can follow it more intelligently, but it has a finer value ; when we take our labor into literature, it is ennobled. Farming has grown steadily in dignity as it has been studied and followed in the light of books. When we read of our pursuits, we think of them more calmly, more profoundly and objectively. Our vocation is so near us that we do not see it, but the book separates us from it, so that we look on all sides. And if by chance it throws about it some ray of genius, — puts it into the setting of a poem or romance, — we go to its tasks with lighter hearts.

(8.) I have no need to suggest that one should read in view of one's deficiencies.

(9.) Read thoroughly. The triteness of the words measures their importance. You may glide over the newspaper and rush through the novel, but have constantly at hand something of a substantial character, and fit to be classed as literature, — a history, a biography, a volume of travels or essays or science, that you are reading for the definite purpose of transferring its contents into your mind, with a view to keeping them there.

Webster said, "Many other students read more than I did, and knew more than I did, but so much as I read I made my own." Burke read a book as if he were never to see it a second time.

(10.) Read from a centre. I mean, take your stand upon an epoch, or character, or question, and read out from it. Suppose it be Iceland : first know the country by books of travel, then study its history through its millenium back to Denmark, then its literature as it runs into Scandinavian romance and mythology, then trace its explorations upon this continent. Suppose it to be Milton : hunt him up and down in the encyclopædias, and wherever else he may be found, from Dr. Johnson's Life, a hundred and fifty years ago, to Pattison's Life, of yesterday. You thus come into a sort of intimacy with your character that is almost personal, and even friendly, if you care so to have it. Or suppose it to be a history : when you come to such a character as Cromwell or Mary Stuart, find out what the various authors say, from the Tory Hume to the radical Froude and the dissenting Geikie. One age, one country, one character, thoroughly mastered — this is reading.

If this seems like making a toil of what should always be a pleasure, let me say that after a time this habit of thoroughness gets to be the source of its keenest enjoyment. We speak of the pleasures of knowledge, but may not have discovered that only *exact* knowledge can yield pleasure. The principle goes very deep. A desultory, careless reader may draw a certain excitement from books, but no peace or satisfaction.

(11.) Having made, by chance, a **deca-logue** of rules, among which I trust there is no useless one, I close with an eleventh commandment, greater than all: Cultivate a friendly feeling towards books.

A great author, Maurice, wrote a volume named " The Friendship of Books." It indicates a very real thing. Milton went so far in giving personality to a book that he said, " Almost as well kill a man as a book." Books are our most steadfast friends ; they are our resource in loneliness ; they go with us on our journeys ; they await our return ; they are our best company ; they are a refuge in pain ; they breathe peace upon our troubles ; they await age as ministers of youth and cheer ; they bring the whole world of men and things to our feet ; they put us in the centre of the world ; they summon us away from our narrow life to their greatness, from our ignorance to their wisdom, from our partial or distempered vision to their calm and universal verdicts. There may be something of discord in their mingled voices, but the undertone **speaks for truth and virtue and faith.**

VIII.

AMUSEMENTS.

Let him not attempt to regulate other people's pleasures by his own tastes." — HELPS.

"And the streets of the city shall be full of boys and girls playing in the streets thereof." — ZECHARIAH.

"I can easily persuade myself, that, if the world were free, — free, I mean, of themselves, — brought up, all, out of work into the pure inspiration of truth and charity, new forms of personal and intellectual beauty would appear, and society itself reveal the Orphic movement." — BUSHNELL.

"The only happiness a brave man ever troubled himself with asking much about was, happiness enough to get his work done." — CARLYLE.

VIII.

AMUSEMENTS.

I WOULD prefer, if it were possible, to avoid entering on the question as to the right or wrong of certain amusements, because I think it a very poor and profitless discussion. It were better to take the subject out of the plane of scruple and allowance, — so far and no farther, this much and no more, — and lift it up into a nobler atmosphere. Instead of haggling over the proper allowance or kind of amusements, I would have one rather indifferent to the whole subject — above it, in short. If you are animated by right principles, and have awakened to the dignity of life, the subject of amusements may be left to settle itself. It is not a difficult, unless it is made a primary, question. When, however, amusements dominate the life; when they consume any considerable fraction of one's time or income; when they are found to be giving a tone to the thoughts; when they pass the line of moderation, and run into excess; when they begin to be in any degree a necessity, having shaped the mind to their form, they grow vexatious, and become a difficult factor in the adjustment of conduct.

There is a famous saying of St. Augustine, " Love and do all things," that covers the subject, though its generalization may be too broad for common use. Still, I hate to descend from the lofty principle that should guide us in the matter to its details. I wish young men were so devoted to their callings that they would feel but slight interest in the technical amusements of the day. I wish they had such a sense of the value of time, when devoted to books, that they would not waste their evenings before minstrel troupes, or in games of any sort. I wish you were so sensitive to place and company that you would avoid billiard saloons. I wish you were so thrifty of money, and so careful of health, and so sensible on several other points, that the all-night ball would be out of question. I wish you had so much of that fine feeling called *aristo-cratic* that you would decline to mingle socially in company that is open to all on payment of money, — a doorkeeper and a ticket the only introduction and barrier. I wish you had so lofty an ambition, such a determination to get on and up in the world, that you would give all these things the go-by for the most.

But these wishes are keyed too high for realization, and I must speak in another way, coming nearer to the casuistry of the subject, though I dislike that view of it. Your demand is for distinctions and drawn lines, and definite rehearsal of the innocent and forbidden. Well, if we make distinctions, let us at least make true ones.

The present perplexity largely comes from accepting, in a hereditary way, distinctions that once may have been necessary, but are so no longer. The amusements and vices of English society under the Stuarts were so interwoven that it was easier to sweep out the whole by a single act of heroic protest than it was to enter upon the nice work of separation. It may have been wise social economy, but it was a mistake to insert this indiscriminate cleansing of society into the fabric of religion. The attitude of the Puritan was, — I will forego all pleasures till

I have crushed out Cavalier vices. It was
so akin to religion that it became identified
with it.   Vices and pleasures were put in
the same category.   There was some justification of Macaulay's remark that the Puritans objected to bear-baiting, not because
it tormented the bear, but because it gave
pleasure to the spectators.   But the stress
that constrained the Puritan passed away,
leaving a set of distinctions as to amusements, all interwoven with religion, but
forming no essential part of it, and having
no basis in clear thought.   Hence all moral
training in New England has had a large
negative element ; its sign has been the *not*
doing certain things.   Meanwhile we have
been learning that our Faith, which ulti-
mately regulates such matters, is not keyed
to such a note, but is a gift, and a spirit that
transforms all things.   Our traditions and
our knowledge have come into conflict.   One
side says, it has always been held wrong to
do this and that, and therefore we must abstain.   The other side denies the binding
force of such logic, and, as always happens
when barriers are thrown down, rushes into
extremes.   On one side is bigotry, on the
other license.   Each mistakes — one in ap-

plying the restrictions of religion to things not essentially evil, the other in forgetting that innocent things may not be the best, and may be used as very bad things. All the grand emphasis of religion, however mistaken, has been on one side, all the eagerness of human nature on the other side. It is not strange that, in such a state of the question, young persons do about as they choose. Truer distinctions will be made when we fully learn that our Faith is not a system of restriction, but a bringer-in of higher life ; not a rule, but an inspiration. When the order and habits of the Faith are established the question of amusements will be a very easy one to settle practically. It tells us that whatever is not in itself evil, whatever is not in excess, whatever does not naturally minister to vice, are free. It does not, however, say that it is best to use this liberty to the full, nor that you are not to come into ways of thinking that shut amusements out of all power to tempt or injure. President-elect Garfield is wholly free to pull in a boat-race, but higher considerations may render it unwise that he should do so; and, having weightier matters on hand, it is not probable that his desires run strongly in that direction.

The debate practically centres upon dancing, cards, and theatre-going. In speaking of them we shall indulge in no equivocation, no paltering with false reasons, no throwing of dust into the eyes in order to gain time, no use of arguments that break down when applied, without essential change, to other things. In illustration, — cards are condemned because they are the tools of gamblers and lead to gambling, but billiards, which are equally the tools of gamblers and are played even less frequently without gambling than cards, have no general and traditional condemnation. Such reasoning and distinctions do infinite harm. Nothing so tends to break down all sense of right and wrong, as basing conduct on false reasons, and making distinctions that are without reasons.

In these three things I think it wiser to discriminate than to reject. I grant that they do not represent very high phases of conduct, and that an atmosphere not the purest invests them; still, it is better to draw the line between use and abuse than to turn them altogether out of life. It may be said that it is easier and safer to reject them, than to apply the distinction. It ought not to be easier to use wrong reason than right reason. All application of truth to society is a matter of faith. It is better to trust an untried truth, than to work a prudential fallacy. Besides, practically, the question has settled itself by usage. Nearly all who feel inclined to do so, dance, and play with cards, and go to the opera and theatre. The circles are very small in which these amusements are totally inhibited; and, in these cases, one is often forced to suspect that the reason of the abstaining lies in their positions rather than in their consciences.

The reason for this almost general indulgence in these amusements is that they are not regarded as essentially evil, or inconsistent with correct principles. It is plainly wiser to make a distinction between use and abuse than to hold fast the door of prohibition after everybody has gone through.

What then of dancing? A very beautiful and simple amusement, based on the mysterious laws of rhythm, — the body responding with the grace of motion to the measure of music. It is not strange that it has been used in religion. So fine a thing, grounded in such sanctity of natural law,

should be kept at the highest point of
beauty and purity.   Any association of it
with what is vile, or coarse, or excessive, is
a profanation.   It is, moreover, as a fine
wine amongst the pleasures, and is not for
daily use.   Its practice is an instruction of
the body, teaching command of the person, and grace and dignity of bearing.   Its
period is in youth, while rhythm has its
seat in the blood, and not after it has passed
into the thought.   Its place is the home,
where parents greet only guests.   So fine a
thing requires the most delicate and gracious ordering.   The hall at which a doorkeeper takes tickets bought in the market,
is plainly not a fit place for a pleasure so
pure and natural, and, because natural, liable
to abuse.   Of all things dancing should not
be miscellaneous.   There can be no objection to visiting a well-conducted circus, but
one should hesitate if it exposed one to an
introduction to the clowns and *equestri-
ennes.*

There are objections of utmost weight to
be urged against the all-night ball.   The
general and unanswerable criticism to be
made upon it is that of *excess.*   The physician, the teacher, the employer, the parent,

the unprejudiced looker-on, each brings in his specific protest. It can be tolerated only as you tolerate a wholesale violation of physical and social laws.

What of card-playing? I suppose if anything could be annihilated without sensible loss to human welfare it would be that small package of paste-board known as cards; but we had best not pray for it lest some worse thing take its place. Their abuse is immense, but they have a use that is at least allowable. An abuse ought not to be suffered to destroy a use, except in rarest cases; it is not the way to prevent evil. The *use* will constantly be clamoring for return, bringing back also the abuse. The wiser way is to separate them by some principles of common sense. In this matter the distinction is easily made. As a household amusement, what can be more innocent? In point of fact, boys, who from the first are accustomed to cards, commonly outgrow them, or hold them as of slightest moment. But stolen bread is sweet, and many a boy has been morally broken down through yielding to well-nigh irresistible temptation to play an innocent game that was prohibited as sinful in his home. There

13

is an amazing lack of practical wisdom in this matter. "I cannot persuade my boys to join me in a game of whist," said a respectable gentleman of his grown-up sons His neighbor forbade cards (I take this twofold note from life) and his four sons grew into gamblers. Gamesters do not come from households in which games are the trivial sports of childhood. Their fascination evaporates with the dew of youth. An amusement in early life, a recreation in age, a thing of indifference in the working period of life, such is the place of cards. Their abuse is very great. As a means of gambling, as a waster of time, as taking the place of rational society, — for a whist-party is an organization of inanity, — they cannot be too sharply condemned.

Young men should govern themselves very strictly in this thing. Don't play in the cars; gamblers do, gentlemen do not, as a rule. Never play in public places, it is the just mark of a loafer. Refuse to devote whole evenings to whist, life is too short and books are too near. Rate the whole matter but lowly, and have such uses for your time and faculties that you can say to others, and to yourself, I have other concerns to attend to.

As to billiards, it is commonly understood that gentlemen sensitive to their surroundings feel obliged to discard them for the most part. In itself a beautiful game, it has been almost impossible to keep it clean and wholesome. Private tables are little used; public saloons are the haunts of well-dressed loafers, and the atmosphere is distinctly charged with small gambling. I have always suspected the title of an eminent physician to his reputation, since I compared the elegance of his billiard-room with the meagreness of his library.

But the war of opinions is waged chiefly over the opera and theatre. If the question were to take the form of indiscrimate and habitual attendance upon them, it would admit of quick answer. There is an old criticism of the stage that is not easily answered. It is twofold; the appeal to the sensibilities is excessive; the scenic cannot be made a vehicle of moral teaching, because the medium is one of unreality,—in ·fine, because it is *acting*. If one were to choose the surest and speediest method of reducing himself to a mush of sensibility let him steadily frequent the opera and theatre. What emotion do they not stir? What

good purpose do they confirm? Hell opens
on the stage and swallows up Don Gio-
vanni, but what *roué* leaves the house with
altered purpose? The play may contain a
moral lesson, but in conveying truth everything depends upon the medium; the worst
possible medium is one that is false. On
the stage nothing is real; everything from
painted scene to costumed actor is fictitious, except the bare sentiment of the
play, which shares the fate of its medium,
and is lost with it behind the last fall of
the curtain.

The claim of the theatre as a school of
morals is false; not because it is immoral,
but because it cannot, from its own nature,
be a teacher of morals. It may have just
claims, but they are not of this sort.

The opera gives us music in nearly the
highest degree of the art. Human society
will never shut itself off from the realization
of any true art, nor ought it to do so. Its
instinctive course is to insist on the art, and
trust to time and change to rid it of evil association. A like claim may be made for
the theatre; it is a field for the expression
of the highest literature through a genuine
art. Here is a solid fact that will never be

wiped out. The stage has stood for three thousand years because it has a basis in human nature. It represents an art, and society never drops an art.

The abuses that have clustered about it are enormous. In evil days it sinks to the bottom of the scale of decency, and in best days it hardly rises to the average. Still, it reflects society, and with the growing habit of attendance it has steadily gained in respectability. A long journey, however, is before it in this direction. " Oh, reform it altogether," prays Hamlet. But the drift is plain, and the final solution is apparent. Society will not drop the stage, but will demand that it shall rise to its own standards, and be as pure as itself ; decent people will have a decent stage.

I have written frankly, because I think it better to give young men the true view of the subject, than to shut them up in prudential inclosures that are full of logical gaps.

It does not by any means follow that it is wise or right for a young man to give himself up to the habit of indiscriminate theatre-going. Aside from moral contamination incident to the average theatre, the influence intellectually is degrading. Its lessons are morbid, distorted, and superficial, they do not mirror life. " Seems, madam," says Hamlet, " I know not seems." Neither do any of us recognize the *seeming* with any power.

But the crucial question comes at last : Shall we never visit the theatre ? When the place is decent in its associations, when the play is pure and has some true worth, when the acting has the merit of art, I know of no principle that forbids it. But if, under these conditions, you see fit to attend, let it be no reason for visiting the average theatre, nor let it represent a habit. The technical amusements should not be made *habits ;* it is recreation — a very different thing — that is to be made habitual.

Our answer provokes the straight question : Would it not be better to make it a matter of rule and principle, and abstain altogether ? We can make rules, but not principles ; they are made for us. The principle here consists in distinguishing between use and abuse, between the bad and the innocent, and not in a blind rejection of the whole matter. As to the rule, it is a nobler and wiser way of treating young men to ask them to observe rational distinctions, than to shut them up to rules they have no mind to observe.

I have said so much on amusements, chiefly in order to get them into a region of clear thought; but I have another and more difficult end in view, namely, to take you altogether away from them, or to lead you to regard them as but trivial and secondary matters. They are not of the substance of life, they do not face the heights of our nature, but are turned toward the child-side of it. The dance, the game, the play, all quite innocent in themselves and involving something of art, are not the stuff out of which manhood is built, nor must they enter largely into it. We naturally connect them with early years, and expect them to drop their claims when life fully asserts itself. It seems not quite in the true order when they largely engage the interest of men and women who are in the midst of their years. Still this is a matter of individual taste and judgment. Dr. Dale of Birmingham tells us of an English fox-hunter who declared that " the keeping of dogs was the noblest of *h*all *h*occupations."

I wage no crusade against these amusements; I am only solicitous lest you rate them too highly, and weigh them too carelessly. It is painful to see a young man of sound conscience in a flutter of question if he may engage in this or that amusement. Diogenes does not long pause over him. Two young men go to their teacher, or some wise friend, for advice; one asks if it is wrong to dance, or play with cards, or go to the theatre. His friend tells him that it is not necessarily wrong to do these things, and, with a word of caution, somewhat sadly sends him away. The other young man asks him if he can put him in the way of getting a list of the Roman emperors, or a fair estimate of Dean Swift, or the various theories of the Great Pyramid, or the "Life of Stephenson," as he has some thought of becoming a railroad man. It needs no prophet to foretell which will be brakeman, and which president of the road.

You have already detected my purpose. It is not to mete the bounds in amusements, but to turn you away from any deep interest in them. They are free to you in a wise way, but you have other business in hand.

It is not without reason that I call you to

the severer estimate of the subject. As matters are going, society seems to be shaping itself into an organization for generating the greatest possible amount of pleasure. The commonest figure to-day — I fear he is almost typical — is the young man demanding, as first of all considerations, that he shall be amused; amused he must be at whatever cost, and if society and education and church are not shaped to that end he will have nought to do with them. Meanwhile church and college and social life hasten to comply, suggesting that the main business of each is to keep up a " show." One wishes with Douglas Jerrold " that the world would get tired of this eternal guffaw." Let me say to the young men who read these pages, that while the many are amusing themselves, a few earnest ones turn aside and seize the prizes of life. I would have you of this number. I would persuade you to extricate yourselves from the giggling crowd, and hold that life may be worth living even if it does not provide you with a stunning amusement every twenty-four hours. I would have you strong and clear-headed enough to enter the protest of your example against the insidious, emasculating idea so prevalent, that the main object in life is " to have a good time." I would have you realize that " a soul sodden with pleasure " is the most utterly lost and degraded soul that can be. When pleasure rules the life, mind, sensibility, health shrivel and waste, till at last, and not tardily, no joy in earth or heaven can move the worn-out heart to response.

But shall a young man have no amusements? He is not shut off from any that sound sense and a high ambition admit of; but if these governing principles are not kept at the fore-front of life, *nothing* is admissible. Just now amusement seems to be primary, while, in truth, it is the last thing about which we need to concern ourselves. What does a bird, or an angel, think of it? Each wings his way, and his flight is his joy.

Mr. Ruskin touches our theme most aptly : " All real and wholesome enjoyments possible to man have been just as possible to him since first he was made of the earth as they are now. To watch the corn grow and the blossoms set, to draw hard breath over plowshare and spade, to read, to think, to love, to hope, to pray; these are the

things that make men happy." Mr. Ruskin
is too lofty, too severe, you say; he is playing his *rôle* of grand grumbler. We find
ourselves after this long discussion simply
exhorted to noble feelings and ambitions,
and left befogged in clouds of high sentiment; life after all is made up of real acts ;
we want to know exactly with what form
of pleasure we may offset our hard toil of
brain or hands, — how we shall let off this
exuberance of vitality that bubbles within,
— how we may gratify this instinct of play
— natural as laughter itself. I will make
what answer I can.

The technical amusements that have been
spoken of,— the stage, the dance, the games,
and things of like nature, — are not to be
regarded as true recreation or play. They
do not rest one, they consume vitality
rather than furnish a channel for it, and
they cannot, from their nature, be closely
enough ingrafted with daily life. They
may serve as an occasional pleasure, but
they cannot afford constant recreation,
which every one must have, and can hardly
have in excess. I would make the broadest and most emphatic distinction between
pleasure derived from these amusements

and *enjoyment* drawn from other sources. I mean, by the distinction, getting our own natures at work in simple and pleasurable ways instead of looking for external excitement.

I may seem to have reached a very prosy conclusion, but I claim that motion in the open air, under clear skies, and in close contact with nature, is the finest and keenest recreation possible to a healthy-minded, full-blooded man. When it is not so regarded it is because neither mind nor body are in normal condition. The distinguishing mark of those who are devoted to the amusements, as contrasted with those who delight in open-air recreation, is *listlessness,* — a very common thing as we note the gait, air, and voice of many young men. The grandest figure of a man seen in Great Britain for a hundred years was Christopher North. In the chapter on *Health* we described him as running amongst the Highlands for hours, exulting in what De Quincey calls " the glory of motion." Wilson knew what pleasure was in other forms, but he knew nothing higher than this — a glorious manhood intoxicated with the wine of overflowing life.

When Dr. Wayland was asked what pleasures he would recommend, he said, " Take a walk." It was not so very prosy advice, nor will it seem so to any one who has not sunk into a prosy state of mind and body. Thoreau considered a walk the height of felicity. My point is, if you would get into close contact with nature and culti‧ vate the intimacies and sympathies that look in that direction, you would win an enjoyment far finer than that to be got from the technical amusements, with their fever‧ ish accessories. Climb the hills about you, — Holyoke, Wachusett, Greylock, the Pali‧ sades. What do you know of the ravines and water-falls within a ten-mile radius? Do you know the haunts and habits of the animals that live in the forests? Do you know the trees, the flowers and their times? Do you know the exultation that comes with standing on mountain tops, and the tender awe that dwells in thick woods and deep glens, and the music of waters in these still heights? And do you know how profound and sweet is sleep after a day in the woods? An hour, or a day, spent in the open air, in saddle, or better, on foot, with cheery company, or alone with an

easy, care-discarding mind, yields recreation that will be satisfying just in the degree in which the nature is sound.

If any say, This is well, but not enough,
or it is not practicable, let me suggest that
they find a *hobby.* There is a provision for
one in nearly every man ; seek it out, and
gratify it wisely. If a horse, let it be that,
steering wide of all jockeying and the vulgarity of the race-course; if animal pets,
nothing is more wholesome. And there
are the athletic sports and the broader field
of art, fine and mechanical, the turning-
lathe, the garden, music, pictures, books,
science, — the keen and unanxious joy of
the amateur awaits you in each.

Every young man, remembering Shakespeare's wise words, " Home-bred youths
have ever homely wits," should now and
then travel. You say traveling is expensive ; but reckon what possibly you may
nave spent the last year in cigars, beer,
balls, theatricals, confectionery, " treats,"
and gew-gaws of dress, and see how far the
sum would have taken you, — to Washington, or Niagara, or Quebec, or London,
perchance.

As our last and weightiest word on the

subject, I would press the distinction between amusements and enjoyment. One is pleasure manufactured and served up for us ; the other is the satisfaction that flows from the sportive action of our own faculties. In other words, amuse yourself instead of depending upon others. Learn the joy of the exercise of your own powers rather than offer yourself to be played upon from without for the sake of a new sensation.

From within out is the order of all life, from smallest plant to man. And because it is the order of life it is also the order of joy.

IX.
FAITH.

"Fecisti nos ad Te, et inquietum est cor nostrum, donec
requiescat in Te." — AUGUSTINE.

"Lord, to whom shall we go? Thou hast the words of eternal life." — (*Said to the Christ.*)

"Blest is the man whose heart and hands are pure!
He hath no sickness that he shall not cure,
No sorrow that he may not well endure :
His feet are steadfast and his hope is sure.

"Oh, blest is he who ne'er hath sold his soul,
Whose will is perfect, and whose word is whole;
Who hath not paid to common-sense the toll
Of self-disgrace, nor owned the world's control!

"Through clouds and shadows of the darkest night,
He will not lose a glimmering of the light;
Nor, though the sun of day be shrouded quite,
Swerve from the narrow path to left or right."
JOHN ADDINGTON SYMONDS.

"If you travel through the world well, you may find cities
without walls, without literature, without kings, moneyless
and such as desire no coin; which know not what theatres or
public halls of bodily exercise mean; but never was there,
nor ever shall there be, any one city seen without temple,
church, or chapel. Nay, methinks a man should sooner find
a city built in the air, without any plot of ground whereon
it is seated, than that any commonwealth altogether void of
religion should either be first established or afterward pre-
served and maintained in that estate. This is that containeth
and holdeth together all human society; this is the foundation,
stay, and prop of all " — PLUTARCH.

IX.

FAITH.

CARLYLE, in that great address of his to the students of Edinburgh, says : " No nation that did not contemplate this wonderful universe with an awe-stricken and reverential feeling that there was a great unknown, omnipotent, and all-wise, and all-virtuous Being, superintending all men in it, and all interests in it — no nation ever came to very much, nor did any man either, who forgot that. If a man did forget that, he forgot the most important part of his mission in this world."

I do not propose in this chapter to do more than follow out the thought of this vigorous utterance.

It will indeed never do to forget " the all-wise, all-virtuous Being " who superintends human society, nor the fact that we have our origin and therefore our destiny in Him. Whether evolution be true or false, or partly

both, men must never doubt that they are
made in the image of God. Hence the Bible
opens with the creation of the world and of
man — the starting-point of philosophy and
religion, as well as of the physical world.
Whether those first pages be regarded as
typical, or figurative, or traditional, or myth-
ical, they are the profoundest and truest
words that we know. No great thinker
treats them slightly ; no man can afford to
forget their personal lesson. They gave
the greatest English poet — after one — his
theme. Milton was no Puritan fanatic turning the crude and harsh theology of his day
into majestic verse, but a seer whose open
eyes rested habitually upon the summits of
truth. Setting himself to the deliberate
task of composing a masterpiece of poetry,
he selected as the greatest possible theme,
the creation of man. Dante wrote of destiny, Milton of origin, and so comprehended
both. Michael Angelo attempted upon canvas the same theme. On the walls of the
Sistine Chapel he strove to tell how man
became a living soul. The created Adam
lies upon a sloping bank in the midst of a
dull and desert solitude — nerveless, lax, an
animal only, waiting for his completion into

man. Above him in the air is the majestic
figure of the Deity whose outstretched hand
touches with one finger the upreaching hand
of Adam, and through the touch, the electric
spark of spiritual life is conveyed, and Adam
becomes a living soul.

The topmost minds of the world do not
repeat this history in poetry and painting
without reason. It is the world's strongest
assertion of the essential oneness of man
with God, — asserted by genius because genius asserts the highest truths. Young men
always revere genius ; each wears something
of the glory of the other. Hence they
should keep in mind that it never speaks
with such unanimity and emphasis as when
it declares the divine origin of man. I find
in a recent novel, a very clear and strong
statement of the incompleteness of man
apart from God. A professor of mathematics upon his dying bed is speaking to a
pupil of great force and talent, who is disposed to push his way in the world without
any recognition of God. The dying mathe-
matician says : " No man is competent to
calculate accurately until he has as perfect
a conception of two-ness as he has of oneness. You cannot estimate things correctly

unless you take into your calculation another
as well as yourself. You are but one in-
teger. Handling, however perfectly, one
factor, your calculations are extremely limited. The other factor is God. Stay, I err,
you are *not* a unit! You are, I am, but zero!
that is, apart from God. Admitting him,
all other factors follow, not otherwise.
Remember what I tell you, this is the sum
of all ; separate quality from quantity, and
your result is wrong ; omit eternity in your
estimate as to area, and your conclusion is
wrong ; fasten your attention exclusively
upon yourself and leave out God, and your
equation is wrong, false, and utterly wrong."

I do not think it is too much to expect
that young men will apprehend these reasons for a positive recognition of God. If
the reasons are profound, they are also
self-asserting. When presented, you say,
I know them already.

> "So close is glory to our dust,
> So near is God to man ;
> When duty whispers low, Thou must,
> The youth replies, I can."

This inner voice, declaring for God and
duty, is often hushed, often unheeded, and
so at last comes to be seldom heard — a

sad and strange thing to happen. I am
aware that young men have a habit of
treating matters of faith in a slighting way,
as not quite lying in the line of manliness.
I will not say that you have not some reason for thinking so. As sometimes presented, it is anything but attractive to a
clear-headed, brave man, — now as a mere
matter of future safety, bare of a single
noble feature; now as a thin and pretty
sentiment, void of all robust thought and
practical duty; now a mesh of doctrinal
subtilties, or a tissue of traditions and dog-
mas. But these phases of the great subject
are rapidly passing away. Whether past
or not, we have only to do with the eternal
truth they obscure. I invite you into the
company of the greatest and best, who
never reject or slight this fact called Christianity; or if any do so it is because of the
pressure of some special adverse influence,
as in the case of Huxley and Clifford and
Spencer — men overweighted with the sci-
entific habit, "dazzled," as Plato said, "by
a too near look at material things," or it is
due to an ill-balanced nature, as in Hume,
who was too cold to feel an emotion. It is
always safe to trust the poets; not much

moral truth has got into the world except
through them, and never have they put the
indorsement of their inspiration upon any
great error. They stand on the highest
summits of life, and therefore see farthest;
they live closest to nature, and therefore
understand her most thoroughly; they are
the fullest endowed with gifts, and therefore best understand man and his needs.
They speak with one voice in this matter.
Lucretius in antiquity, — a naturalist rather
than a poet, — and Shelley in modern times,
a man preternaturally sensitive to falseness
and so repelled by the hypocrisy of his age;
— these are nearly the only unbelievers
amongst the poets. Put by the side of Lucretius, Wordsworth, who seems to have
written no line except in that Presence

> " Whose dwelling is the light of setting suns,
>   And the round ocean and the living air
>   And the blue sky, and in the mind of man ; "

or by the side of Shelley, the not only finer
but more robust Tennyson, who prefaces
the greatest of modern poems with prayer
to the —

> " Strong Son of God, immortal Love."

It is a fact of immense significance that the
poets thus bow with reverence before the

Christian faith; for the poet is a seer; it is his gift and function to declare *the reality of things.* Now Christianity, in its broadest definition, is simply the reality of things. It is a setting forth of the true order of humanity. When a man grasps this secret, he must accept Christianity. He does violence to himself if he refuses.

I have all along in these pages had in mind those who have begun to think. I ask you to think here — not alone, nor yet with any sect — but with the great souls. If they are mistaken, if they see amiss, the whole world is blind.

But if, intellectually, we are forced to accept the Christian idea, we must carry it into the conscience where we encounter that word which Carlyle declares to be the mightiest of all words — *ought,* and by which convictions are transmuted into duties. You cannot build a wall about your logical and critical faculties and say, " Here will I entertain my faith." There can be no wall, nor line even, between the intellect and the moral nature. When universal truths like those of Christianity come to man they spread throughout his whole being. Intellectual conviction means moral

assent. The conviction sweeps like a wind
into every recess of his nature and sets to
vibrating those chords that declare the *ought*
of duty. And so we are borne on to the
higher sentiments of love and adoration and
spiritual sympathy. If there is a God, I
must love him. I must pour out my soul
upon him. I must worship at his feet. I
must be at one with him. The logic of our
nature, with tender but relentless force,
drives us to this final issue.

> " When duty whispers low, Thou must,
>   The youth replies, I can."

(1.) My first practical suggestion in regard to faith is that you treat it *earnestly*
and never otherwise. If you have wit to
scatter broadly, withhold it from this theme.
No sound nature ever makes a mock of it.
Your true-hearted, fine-grained man puts
off his shoes at the door of a mosque as
devoutly as any Moslem; he treads the
aisles of a cathedral as softly as any Ro-
manist; he despises no incense; he sneers
at no idol. He may deny, but he will not
jest. The sneer is crucial; bring one who
indulges in it to the test and you will find
him crude in thought and coarse in feeling.
I know how common it is and how much

there is to provoke it in the humanly-weak forms of worship and eccentricities of belief; still, the most deluded Seventh-day Baptist, or Sandemanian literalist, ranks higher than one who scoffs at them. I like to hear one pronounce the name of God with a subdued awe, and to see the cast of thought overspread the features when eternal things are named. I like to see a delicate and quiet handling of sacred truths — as you speak the name of your mother in heaven. I might say that this is the way a gentleman bears himself towards religion, but I would rather have you feel that it is the treatment due to the majesty of the subject.

(2.) If you happen to be skeptical, do not formulate your doubts, nor regard them as convictions. Doubt is almost a natural phase of life; but as certainly as it is natural is it also temporary, unless it is unwisely wrought into conduct. The chief danger is lest one, blinded and confused by the " excess of light " with which life dawns, may come to think that one is not amenable to the laws of morality; that, having no chart or compass, he may drift with the tides. This is not good moral seamanship When storms have swept away compass and quadrant and chart, the sailor still steers the ship and watches for some opening in the clouds that may reveal a guiding star; he scans the waters for sight of some fellow voyager, and at night listens for the possible roar of breakers, and so, by re-doubling his seamanship at all points, finds at length his course. When one finds himself in this skeptical mood, he should govern himself in the strictest manner, using whatever of truth and moral sense he has left with utmost fidelity, doing the one thing that he still knows to be right. One may doubt, and the whole apparatus of his moral nature remain sound; if one works that aright, one cannot long remain astray. There is wonderful light-generating power in good conduct. "I am skeptical; therefore I have nothing to do with Bible or church or sermon; I am skeptical, therefore I am not bound to the moral courses taught by religion; I am skeptical, therefore, having no faith or law, I will be a law unto myself;" — this is both poor thinking and bad morality. Skepticism by its nature as simply *doubt*, as not even negation, requires that it should not be made a rule or reason for conduct. It may possibly be rational to

act from a negation, but not from a doubt.
It is worse than building upon the sand; it
is building on chaos.

It is well to remember, as Plutarch tells
us on the prefatory page of the chapter,
that nothing so universally engages the attention of men as religion; hence, nothing
will bear so long study. Its final verdicts
are reached only through experience. A
young man pronounced in unbelief is premature; he has decided that Jupiter has no
moons without waiting to look through a
telescope. The experience of life nearly
always works towards the confirmation of
faith. It is the total significance of life
that it reveals God to man; and life only
can do this; — neither thought, nor demonstration, nor miracle, but life only, weav-
ing its threads of daily toil and trial and
joy into a pattern on which at last is in-
scribed the name, God. It is a fact of immense significance that Emerson, who in
early years looked askance at this name,
suffers himself, in his old age, to be called
a Christian theist. I ask young men to
wait and hear what life has to say before
they formulate their doubts. The years
have a message for you that you must not
fail to hear.

(3.) Be intelligent in regard to Christianity.

An eminent American statesman, though
an unbeliever, daily read the Bible, on the
ground that every citizen should be familiar
with the religion of his country. Had he
gone a step farther and read it because it
contained the religion of the civilized world,
he would have read from a higher consideration, and perhaps to better purpose. For
this faith marches at the head of the army
of progress. It is found beside the most
refined life, the freest government, the profoundest philosophy, the noblest poetry, the
purest humanity. I think we are all of us
bound to have a clear conception of this
fact that thus possesses and dominates human society. I do not think it too much to
expect of young men that they shall know
its external history, and from that go on and
raise the question, What is the secret of the
power of Christianity? Why does it lay
strongest hold of the best races? Why
does it pave the way to freedom and social
elevation? Why does it make a man better? Why does it have the peculiar effect
of ennobling and dignifying character?
What is the subtle power by which it

breathes peace upon troubled hearts? Why does it make the path of daily duty an easy one to tread? What is it that makes the epithet *Christian* mean the best of its kind, whether applied to a civilization, to a community, to individual conduct, or to an inward temper? Not long ago a ship was wrecked upon the reefs of an island in the Pacific. The sailors, escaping to land, feared lest they might fall into the hands of savages. One climbed a bluff to reconnoitre; — turning to his mates, he shouted, " Come on, here 's a church; " — a simple story, but involving a profound question, Why was it safer for shipwrecked men to go where a church upreared its cross than where there was none?

(4.) I go a step farther when, for the same reasons, I urge upon you a study of the character of Jesus Christ.

It is almost a modern thing, this analysis and measurement of that divine Person. In former days, when religious thought took chiefly theological forms, the Christ was but a factor of a system; but since we have begun to think from more practical stand-points, the question has arisen, What sort of a man was Christ? Dr. Bushnell, in the famous tenth chapter of his book, " Nature and the Supernatural," first made the question a general one in this country. In England, it had found place in the writings of Coleridge, Dr. Arnold, Maurice, Robertson, and others of their school of thought. It became popular through " Ecce Homo," and is to-day the favorite theme of religious speculation, as shown in Phillips Brooks's " Influence of Jesus," and in Thomas Hughes's " Manliness of Christ." Led by such teachers as these, you find that you have before you a character more curiously interesting, more wonderful than any other that history can show. You find that you cannot classify him, — elusive and passing out of sight on some sides of his character, yet most near and tangible on other sides, — a Jew, yet not Jewish, — of the first century and equally of all centuries, — an idealist, but not transcending possibility ; a reformer, but not a destroyer ; making for the first time what is highest in character, the most effective in action, — a true full member of the common humanity, but transcending it till he is one with God, a being at the same time so weak that he can die, and so strong that he is superior to death, a person at once so near and human that we call him our brother, and so high and mysterious that we bow at his feet as our Lord and Master.

Now, no thoughtful person can get beyond the first superficial look at this Jesus, without ever after holding him in highest veneration. Nor can one study this character long without perceiving that it contains the true order of humanity, and "points the way we are going" to the end of time. Nor can we long contemplate the Christ without feeling his personality pressing upon ours with transforming power.

(5.) Allow full play to the sense of accountability.

When Daniel Webster was Secretary of State under President Fillmore, he was invited to a dinner at the Astor House with about twenty gentlemen. He seemed weary with his journey, and, speaking but little, if at all, sank into a sort of reverie, out of keeping with the occasion. All other attempts at conversation failing, a gentleman out to him this strange question: "Mr. Webster, will you tell me what was the most important thought that ever occupied your mind?" Mr. Webster slowly passed his hand over his forehead, and in a low tone said to one near him, "Is there any one here who does not know me?" "No; all are your friends." "The most important thought that ever occupied my mind," said Mr. Webster, "was that of my individual responsibility to God!" upon which he spoke to them for twenty minutes, when he rose from the table and retired to his room.[1]

It is the most important thought, because it pertains to our highest relation. It ushers in that sum of all duties, — *fidelity*. It is the only thought that can move our whole nature and move it aright. Pleasure and ambition and self-respect touch us on this side and on that, but they do not invest us with an all-embracing purpose, as does this sense of "individual responsibility to God." There are noble motives and passions that bear us to noble conclusions in conduct and character, but only this lifts us to the height of our being. "God made us for Himself," says Augustine, "and we have no rest till we find rest in Him."

(6.) Have for yourself definite religious duties and relations.

I think you all understand very well that

---

[1] Mr. Harvey's *Reminiscences*, page 403.

the common talk about respecting religion
is of very little moment, apart from conduct.
Whatever other mistake you make in respect to religion, don't patronize it. This
is a very matter-of-fact world, and religion
is the most matter-of-fact thing in it. The
hard common sense of the matter is that a
practical relation to faith is the only real
and vital relation to it. I am at the farthest from hinting under what name you
should worship; I only say that reason requires that you kneel at some altar, and
that you confess in some real way your belief " in the communion of saints." To get
the good of other relations, you fulfill them.
To learn good manners, you mingle in
society. To secure a fair name, you tell
the truth and maintain your honor. If you
belong to a club, or lodge, or board of direct-
ors, you meet its appointments. Do not
regard the external forms of faith with less
intelligent logic.

I have no fear that you will think I summon you to other than the most manly view
of life when I urge the religious view of it.

We have linked our themes at many
points with the testimony of the great minds
whose inspiration it is the glory of your

youth that you feel and respond to. They speak as emphatically here as elsewhere.

When Walter Scott was approaching his end, he said to Lockhart, "I may have but a minute to speak to you. My dear, be a good man, — be virtuous, — be religious, — be a good man. Nothing else will give you any comfort when you come to lie here;" — a pensive testimony, but how tender and honest!

All critical thought agrees that in Hamlet we have not only the profoundest but the most personal thought of Shakespeare. It is hard to resist the feeling that in the following lines he struck deeper than the artist, and revealed a personal conviction and experience. At least, he knew what a man will do who has sounded life, and caught sight of his work.

> " And so, without more circumstance at all,
> I hold it fit that we shake hands, and part;
> You, as your business and desire shall point you —
> For every man has business and desire,
> Such as it is, — and for mine own poor part,
> Look you, *I 'll go pray.*"